Shoreline of Infinity

Issue 8½ Summer 2017

Science fiction magazine from Scotland

Special Edition

In partnership with

Edinburgh International Book Festival

Shoreline of Infinity Science Fiction Magazine is published in Edinburgh. It features short fiction, articles, poetry, art, reviews and more. The first issue was published in the summer of 2015; already we have published some astonishingly good stories from new and more well known writers, from Scotland and from around the world.

We also run a monthly science fiction cabaret, *Event Horizon*.

Shoreline *of* Infinity

Issue 8½ Summer 2017

Science fiction magazine from Scotland

ISBN 978-1-9997002-1-8

Shoreline of Infinity is available in digital or print editions.
Submissions of fiction, art, reviews, poetry, non-fiction are welcomed:
visit the website to find out how to submit.

www.shorelineofinfinity.com

Publisher
Shoreline of Infinity Publications / The New Curiosity Shop
Edinburgh
Scotland
280717

Contents

Cover: *Stuart Beel*

Editorial Team

Editor & Editor-in-Chief:
Noel Chidwick

Art Director:
Mark Toner

Deputy Editor & Poetry Editor:
Russell Jones

Reviews Editor:
Iain Maloney

Assistant Editor & First Reader:
Monica Burns

Copy editors:
Iain Maloney, Russell Jones, Monica
Burns, Andrew J Wilson

Extra thanks to:
Caroline Grebbell, M Luke McDonell,
Katy Lennon, Abbie Waters

First Contact
www.shorelineofinfinity.com
contact@shorelineofInfinity.com
Twitter: @shoreinf
and on Facebook

Pull Up a Log

Walking Naked Through Your Old School

Ken MacLeod

There's a widespread misconception that science fiction succeeds best when it predicts the future. Most if not all SF writers and readers would scoff at the notion. We don't write and read the stuff to see what the future will be like. We read it for entertainment and enlightenment. Futures we know will never happen (because science has moved on, or the supposed date of the story – 1984, say – is already past) can still engage us. We'll never meet the Martians of Wells, of Burroughs, of Bradbury, of Heinlein… but we greet them on the page nevertheless.

But strangely, it matters to us that the writers were sincere in their expectation, or (in some late cases, such as Roger Zelazny in his tales set on Mars and Venus) ironic about its falsity. It's part of the genre's bargain with the reader, first struck in the preface to Mary Shelley's Frankenstein, that this be so. Otherwise, we have fantasy, and a different bargain.

(Or we have Hollywood – but SF in other media – film, television, gaming – is a whole other bargain, and best judged in its own terms.)

The writers I've had the privilege and pleasure of selecting for the SF strand in this year's Edinburgh International Book Festival are all very conscious of what they're doing when they write science fiction, and when they write about it. Stephen Baxter has taken hard SF to the limit and beyond, and

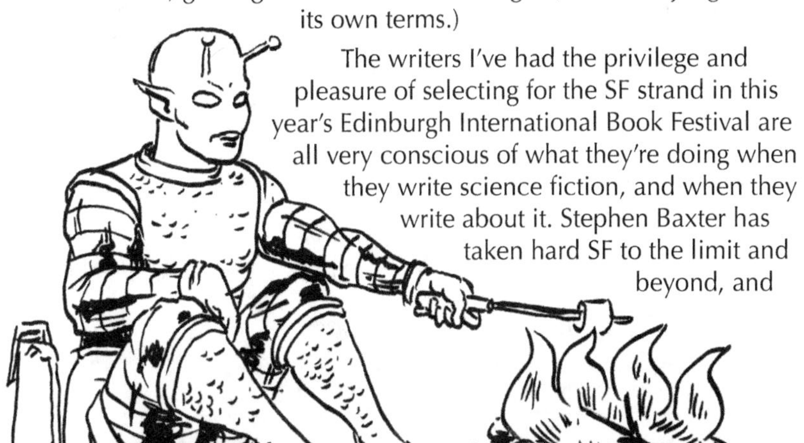

branched out into alternate and retro-SF history. (I look forward to meeting his Wellsian Martians, back for a second swing at us.) Nalo Hopkinson has combined Caribbean and cosmic perspectives, to striking and disquieting effect. Ada Palmer has recently burst on the scene with an intricate trilogy set in a grounded future history, a world as strange to us as ours would be to Leonardo. Jo Walton is a wise critic and voracious reader (and indeed re-reader) with SF's past at her fingertips and its future in her grasp, her own novels diverse and assured. Adam Roberts likewise combines criticism and creation, with an alarmingly fast-growing body of work that never repeats itself. And our own Charles Stross, very much of Edinburgh and Scotland, has so many and varied series to his name that a cross-section covers most current kinds of SF.

Scotland has a flourishing SF and fantasy scene, whose writers can look to distinguished predecessors such as Robert Louis Stevenson, Naomi Mitchison, David Lindsay, Edwin Morgan and Alastair Gray, whose work may have been innocent of commercial genre but which planted the fantastic and scientific sensibility firmly in the national literature. Iain Banks, much missed and mourned, carried that flag forward and directly inspired many of us.

SF can't, as I've said, predict the future, but it can shape it. In strange times like these, it provides us with our anxiety dreams, our nightmares, our fantasies. The purpose of these off-line activities of the sleeping brain is not premonitory, but admonitory – they tell us to get on with it, to meet the challenges of the day. SF at its best can do the same.

Ken MacLeod was born in Stornoway, Isle of Lewis, Scotland and lives in Inverclyde. He has Honours and Masters degrees in biological subjects and worked for ten years in the IT industry. Since 1997 he has been a full-time writer. He is the author of sixteen novels, from *The Star Fraction* (1995) to *The Corporation Wars: Insurgence* (Orbit, Nov 2016), and many articles and short stories. His novels and stories have received three BSFA awards and three Prometheus Awards, and several have been short-listed for the Clarke and Hugo Awards. He has just completed a space opera trilogy with *The Corporation Wars: Emergence* (forthcoming Sept 2017).
He is Guest Selector for the SF strand at the 2017 Edinburgh International Book Festival.
Ken MacLeod's blog is The Early Days of a Better Nation
http://kenmacleod.blogspot.com
His twitter feed is @amendlocke

From the Editor's Log

Noel Chidwick

This year, Ken MacLeod was asked to invite acclaimed SF writers to talk at the Edinburgh International Book Festival, and we were asked to host an Event Horizon sci-fi cabaret night in the Unbound tent.

"Why not produce a special edition of *Shoreline of Infinity* for the Book Festival?" EIBF asked. Why not indeed. Our thanks go to the EIBF for their full support for this project. So, here are the results:

We have fantastic sci-fi stories, articles and poems from Pippa Goldschmidt, Adam Roberts, Ken MacLeod, Ada Palmer, Nalo Hopkinson, Charles Stross, Jo Walton and Jane Yolen (all of whom are appearing at the Book Festival). Our thanks go to Ken for twisting his guests' arms for this issue (though this seems to have been more a nudge, so willingly did they provide their pieces, so big thanks to them as well).

This issue also shows off some of the fine Scottish science fiction talent we have been privileged to publish. Tips of the hat go to: Caroline Grebbell, Iain Maloney, Russell Jones, Dee Raspin, Gary Gibson, Thomas Clark, Katie Gray and Andrew J Wilson for their stories. We are also delighted to use this issue as an excuse to re-publish Ruth EJ Booth's BSFA award winning story, The Honey Trap. Ruth writes a regular well-loved column on the boulder-strewn path to becoming a writer.

This special issue is also an opportunity for the editorial team to reflect. Iain Maloney, takes a look at Scottish dystopian fiction, Russell Jones talks about SF poetry and, as MC and organiser, tells us about Event Horizon. Monica Burns brings us up to date with SF Caledonia, our project on early Scottish science fiction, and Mark Toner explores the artwork of Shoreline of Infinity.

If this special edition has given you a taste of what we do, and you want more, all our back issues are available from

www.shorelineofinfinity.com

Now, we invite you to turn the page and step into exciting new tides on the *Shoreline of Infinity*…

First published in Shoreline of Infinity 4

The Stilt-Men of the Lunar Swamps

Andrew J. Wilson

Art: Stephen Pickering

I. Introductions Are Made

The yarn I'm about to tell you had almost spun itself out by the time I picked up the thread. Still, I was very lucky to have heard it at all, and in the end, I too got to play a small part in the story of the stilt-men of the lunar swamps.

I was enjoying a nightcap in the faded splendour of New York City's Weckquaesgeek Hotel when a garrulous drunk drew my attention. The red-faced man trying to cadge yet more liquor from the other patrons of the bar was, I realised, none other than Donald "Bud" Franklin. His slurred words grew louder as his temper flared, and it became clear that the Korean War veteran and former lunar astronaut was about to make a scene. Franklin climbed unsteadily onto a table, then bent over and dropped his trousers, shouting, "Here's two moons for the price of one, ya goddam rubberneckers!"

He'd been caught in a downward spiral since leaving the Apollo programme, and had finally reduced himself to the level of a side-show freak. But this was only the beginning of Big Bad Bud's performance, and his audience were in for much more than they'd bargained for that evening.

"Now," he yelled between his legs, "since y'all are so interested in what it was like, I'll give ya a practical demonstration of a Saturn V launch!" Then he waved a Zippo lighter around his buttocks and broke wind.

In the ensuing chaos, I spotted a small and elegant old woman who remained unperturbed. There was something familiar about her wrinkled face, as well as the way she calmly smoked pastel-coloured Balkan Sobranies in a stylish cigarette holder. When she realised that I'd been watching her, she beckoned me over to her table.

"Did you know that GI Bud Franklin is an anagram of 'blinking fraud'?" Her pleasantly raspy voice and inimitable turn of phrase told me who she was.

"Madam, I'm honoured," I said.

"But you *had* assumed I was dead, yes?"

She was, as ever, quite correct.

"Don't concern yourself, young man. Even I have to scan the obituaries every morning to reassure myself that I'm still in the land of the living."

Ursula Underhill was one of the greatest wits and finest literary stylists of her generation. I was so pleased to be in her presence that I'd almost completely forgotten about Franklin's idiocy until the security guards blundered past us, the former astronaut and his abandoned trousers clamped firmly in their sweaty hands.

"It's tragic, really," Ursula sighed, "but then the poor soul never saw the real Moon. Perhaps things might have been different if he had."

"I beg your pardon?"

"Oh, I was there years before all that NASA hoo-hah."

I stared at her in consternation, worried that she might be rambling with senility – and taken aback by her pronunciation of the acronym of the National Aeronautics and Space Administration as "Nassau".

"Don't look at me like that, young man… otherwise, I won't give you the story of a lifetime!"

II. The Professor's Exposition

You see, young man, even for a woman of my meagre talents, it was something of a disappointment to be relegated to the role of gossip columnist. I had arrived in England determined to make my mark as a social and political commentator. However, I rapidly found that all I could place were trivial sketches of the idle and the vain. These were times when men were men, and quite frankly, my dear, women were appalled.

You're too young to have heard of Montgomery Montgolfier Monk, big game hunter, self-styled adventurer and would-be lady killer. His monogram was MMM, and he insisted that it should be pronounced "mmm". The oaf thought it charming to whisper in the shell-like ears of debutantes that he was just a big sweetie, hard on the outside but soft within. Soft in the head was more like it, and I found his syrupy sayings more sickly than sweet. He was the kind of man who put the "ass" in passion.

Still, Monty Monk must have decided that I was a challenge to be scaled like one of his mountains, or bagged like some poor beast of the jungle. He fed me titbits for my columns, and introduced me to the eccentric orbit of a gang of socialites who were, Lord help me, even ghastlier and more ridiculous than him. I tolerated his persistence, and he eventually introduced me to his godfather, Professor Festus MacGuffin.

It must have been late in the autumn of nineteen thirty-two when Monty drove me down to the professor's estate in Berkshire. He had spun me a line about a great news story, and obviously thought he was going to be able to hook me with this so-called scoop and then reel me in over the course of the weekend. I was very much on my guard for the whole journey, but as we drove through the heavily wooded grounds, I realised that Triple-M might have inadvertently made my career.

Standing on the lawns screened by the trees was what I can only describe as an enormous steel sieve. I could not imagine the purpose of such an eyesore, but Monty assured me that it would be the sensation of the age before making it obvious that he had no idea what it was either.

We were met at the door by a neat young Oriental, whom Monty introduced as Kong.

"The professor is expecting you," the Chinaman told us with hardly a trace of any accent. "Dinner will be at eight, and your host will be pleased to demonstrate his latest invention immediately afterwards."

MacGuffin was one of the last surviving gentleman scientists, that enthusiastic species of amateur investigator who had flourished in the Victorian age. Now in his seventies, he combined bookish erudition with the manners of a country squire. His patriarchal beard was so bushy it looked as if he had tried to swallow a baby badger, but failed miserably in the attempt.

"Y'see, m'dear," he told me over the roast pheasant, "I've cracked the problem at last – I can now remotely observe the farthest parts of the world, all from the comfort of m'own study, don't y'know! The

Omniscope is a window on the world, and perhaps on other spheres as well…"

By the time the men were on to the port and cigars, I had listened to a barely coherent monologue about the technical details, which had gone over my head, out the door and all the way to Timbuktu. Monty had revelled in every word, but by the vacant look on his face, he had made even less sense of it than myself. The boob was simply taking childish delight in the sound of big words like 'selenography' and 'phlogiston'. Even the professor seemed to lose his thread half the time, and was compelled to ask Kong for clarification as the taciturn Oriental waited on us.

The Chinaman's moustache hung like quotation marks around the proverbially inscrutable slash of his mouth as he murmured definitions or ironed out details. Not only was Kong master chef, *maître d'* and chief bottle-washer for MacGuffin, I began to suspect that he was also quite probably the man who had built the Omniscope too.

"Come on, godparent, let's see the bally thing in action then!" Monty said at last, and we all trooped down the hall to the study.

A projection screen filled one whole wall. A veritable spaghetti Bolognese of wiring connected this apparatus to a brass control unit, which was, in turn, hooked up to the gigantic sieve on the other side of the partially open French windows.

"You do the honours, Kong," the professor said, and the whole lash-up was switched on. A wavering image came slowly into focus, and we realised that we were looking at ourselves.

"Have I put on weight?" bleated Monty as he saw himself from behind, but everyone else ignored him as Kong tweaked the controls. The screen blurred again and we saw London Bridge.

"The Taj Mahal next, I think!" the professor commanded, and so it was. People and places were paraded before us, and I, for one, was completely captivated by this novel magic lantern show. Unfortunately, Monty had an attention span so short it couldn't form a bridge across the space between his ears.

"Seen it before, been there, done that," he rambled irritatingly after only a few minutes.

"Gadzooks, lad! Are y'tired of the grand tour already?" the professor retorted and turned to his assistant. "Go on, Kong, pull out all the stops!"

The picture was wiped blank in a trice and only a few spangles of light broke the velvety darkness. Then the Moon loomed into view like a great, mottled balloon. The perspective lurched sickeningly, and the grey face of the rocky ball swelled to fill the screen.

"It looks a little arid," I remarked dryly as the seas, craters and ridges of our satellite became ever larger and more detailed.

"Wait, m'dear," the professor cautioned. "Although this airless waste is the lunar surface, it's only one part of it…"

A vast and seemingly bottomless crater came into view. Then our viewpoint plunged into the darkened well, and the sides of the shadowy pit slipped past at extreme speed. Eventually, stars pinpricked the darkness at what I imagined should have been the bottom of the enormous shaft, and I was amazed to find that the tunnel ran right through the core of our satellite.

"Now we'll be the first people to see the dark side of the Moon," the professor crowed with glee. "Then to the lunar pole, Kong!"

More drab and lifeless territory flashed past until we were confronted by a gigantic ice-ringed pit that punctured the roof of the Moon. For a moment, as if by pre-arrangement, the vertiginous motion ceased and Kong took his hands from the controls of the Omniscope. The professor lit his pipe as I struggled to catch up with my shorthand notes, then he addressed the room.

"Dear lady and gentlemen, not only have we proved the worth of the Omniscope, I've accomplished the main task for which it was designed!" Kong applauded politely as Monty and I glanced at each other in confusion. "Many astronomers have recently maintained that the Moon is a barren desert with no atmosphere worth speaking of – a celestial Slough, if you will. Their understandable error has been founded on astronomical observations of only one part of the lunar exterior. They would say one half of the surface, but I now argue that their telescopes can view even less. For, y'see, the Moon is a Klein bottle – a Möbius strip spun into three dimensions – a satellite with a single surface that can be exposed to vacuum on what previous observers have mistakenly described as its 'outside', but one that may sustain an entirely different environment within!"

My astonishment at what had gone before was made redundant by what happened next. Kong manipulated the levers, and our perspective plummeted into the vast hole yawning in the pockmarked surface. Far from the Stygian tunnel that we had observed previously, we were shown a realm of cloudy luminescence as our bird's-eye view drifted into the hidden realm.

"Just as I thought, m'boy!" the professor chortled as he nudged the dazed-looking Monty into alertness again. "The Moon does have an atmosphere – on the inside! And there's light too. Any thoughts, Kong?"

"I would hazard a guess that phosphorescence from minerals, or even rudimentary life forms, could be responsible for the illumination we can see, Professor," his assistant replied.

"Rudimentary?" I asked incredulously as the cloud cover broke and an extraordinary landscape became visible. Life burgeoned within the Moon: corkscrew trees with indigo foliage erupted from a swamp that steamed like primordial soup; things with leathery wings swooped over the forest snapping at iridescent insects of every shape and size; and down in the mire, massive eels coiled through the waters – or perhaps these were just the tentacles of some even more mind-boggling beast.

Wonder followed wonder in this subterranean bayou. Then we came upon the things that walked like men, but even more like men on stilts. Their extraordinarily long legs allowed these prodigies of nature to stride unhindered across the turbid waters of their world, while great flapping ears like those of elephants seemed to act as balancing mechanisms. In other respects, the creatures seemed almost human. They even wore simple, roughly made clothes, including huge puffy hats, and carried tools which looked surprisingly sophisticated.

"That one, Kong," the professor barked. "Let's take a closer look at this fellow and see what he's got in his three-fingered hands."

Monty had wandered right up to screen, as if mesmerised by the images. "It looks like he's got some kind of camera in his mitts. Golly, you can almost smell the swamp water… In fact, you can almost smell the blighter himself –"

Things became somewhat confused at this point.

As the Omniscope zeroed in on the stilt-man, the creature started in surprise, folded his face in a frown, and jerked the lens of his own contraption in what seemed to be our direction. There was a bang as several of the valves on the console exploded. Then, accompanied by an audible pop, the stilt-man reached *through* the screen and grabbed a flabbergasted Monty Monk by the ears. It was a moment's work for the Man-in-the-Moon to haul the man about town through the window made by the Omniscope – and into the strange new world on the other side.

At this point, the power failed and the professor's study was plunged into darkness. Three things were audible: Monty's fading squeals of "Oh, I say!"; the professor's inventive but unprintable profanity; and someone or something yelling, "Kumquats! Hose-pipe! Banana peel!"

III. A Surprising Development

As soon as the lights had flickered on again, Kong set about repairing what I now regarded as *his* machine. Once the spent valves were replaced, the view of the now-deserted lunar swamps came back into focus. The professor repeatedly poked a shooting stick through the Omniscope's screen to confirm that the weird portal remained open, and we hatched a Curate's egg of a plan.

MacGuffin gathered together the rest of his staff and assembled an arsenal of small arms and hunting rifles. The French windows were opened wide, and the servants hauled a small motor launch – commandeered from a nearby lake – along the drive, through the study and up to the screen, before plunging it into the waters of the lunar interior. Finally, Kong, the professor and I – all now changed into outdoor clothing – clambered through the omniscopic window and into the boat. The lower lunar gravity made the transition difficult, but reassuringly increased our strength in that curious place.

Looking back at our point of entry, I was disoriented by the sight of the portal hanging in mid-air. It was as if a magical knife had cut a rectangular hole in reality, peeling away a slice of the lunar landscape to reveal the professor's crowded study. One could even have fancied that the scene was only a cleverly rendered *trompe-l'œil*, if not for the busy movements of the servants within. Queerer still was the effect created when Kong piloted our boat around the portal, for there was no back to the gateway! We found that our egress only existed in one dimension: there was no discernible edge to the thing, and our views of the steaming lunar interior were uninterrupted once we had positioned ourselves to the rear.

Such riddles could have occupied us for days, but that was time we could ill afford to spend in contemplation when we had a blue-blooded buffoon to rescue. Kong gunned the engine and the launch surged forward, taking us towards our unsolicited appointment with destiny.

It was only once we were moving that the professor remembered that I was a woman.

"Good God, we can't take you with us, gel – this is no place for a lady. Kong, turn this boat around!"

I was about to argue when Kong replied for me.

"I believe that Miss Underhill was one of the leading markswomen in the ladies' shooting club when she attended Harvard, sir."

MacGuffin stared at me as I nodded frostily, adding, "One doesn't like to boast." The matter was settled when I pointedly plucked a large log from the water and crushed it with my bare hands. "What's more, I no longer appear to be a member of the weaker sex in this sphere."

Kong steered the boat in a broad circle through the mauve and heliotrope foliage. The purplish world around us exploded with life as we passed. Most of the bizarre creatures around us fled from the noise, fumes and surging wake of our boat, and the rest recoiled from sharp blows from the professor's shooting stick.

The air was heavy with humidity and the overpoweringly spicy odours of the swamp. High above us, thick cumuli boiled around a nebulous source of light. Some of these clouds seemed to break apart into smaller clumps, and these floated downwards in a distinct direction. Although we saw no stilt-men, the drifting clouds pointed us towards what had to be their stronghold.

A great spiral tower rose out of the swamps, beckoning us like an index finger signalling to a lackadaisical waiter. We certainly intended to give the Moon-men something to chew on, but I, for one, was not out to serve up any dish as cold as revenge. Rather, I wanted to spare the stilt-men from sampling too much of their entrée – Monty Monk was hardly a good appetiser for our civilisation. To be frank, he was enough to give anybody indigestion.

"We'll give 'em Hell for kidnapping m'godson, won't we, m'dear?" MacGuffin growled. "Two crack shots should be enough to settle their hash. Course Kong here won't touch firearms because of his religion, but he's a master of Carrot or Judy, one of those Oriental martial arts."

"With all due respect, I think we should be careful, Professor," I replied. "After all, the stilt-man may have just been as curious as we were. We don't know he meant any harm."

"Well, he acted as if he was up to no good – I say we take no chances, no prisoners and no lip!"

"If I may, Professor," Kong interjected, "let me agree with Miss Underhill's suggestion that we employ a modicum of caution in our dealings with these creatures."

"Why, man? Tell me why we should give these savages anything more than the hiding they deserve."

Kong visibly held his tongue for a moment, then composed himself before continuing.

"Because, Professor, they can hardly be counted as savages…"

MacGuffin snorted like a surfacing walrus.

"Balderdash, man, how else would you describe the beggars?"

"I wouldn't care to hazard a guess without further data, sir, but one thing is certainly clear – they're advanced enough to have developed their own equivalent of the Omniscope."

"Hogwash!"

"That can be the only explanation for our present predicament. You will remember that the creature who took Mister Monk was using a device when we first caught sight of him, a device he turned in our direction…"

I did indeed recall the camera-like apparatus that the stilt-man had been operating, as did the professor, if his wordless grumble was anything to go by.

"I surmise that it has to be a mechanism very like our own. That can be the only explanation for the tear in the fabric of space. We observed him as he turned his own Omniscope in our direction and the beams of the two devices interfered with each other, creating the disruption that has bridged the gap between our two worlds…"

"Oh," said the professor succinctly before qualifying this pearl of wisdom with a superfluous, "Ah."

The debate was obviously at an end.

Kong sent the launch hurtling into a broad channel lined with the corkscrew trees. It seemed to lead straight to the cyclopean tower.

"Let us all be on our guard," he warned as we cocked our weapons.

Then some of the tree trunks moved in the water, and I realised that we were surrounded by hooting stilt-men who had hidden their upper bodies in the thick foliage.

"Hell's teeth!" the professor bellowed, but their nets were upon us as he cried out. Our launch remained spinning in the water as we were hauled upwards in the sticky mesh. Even though we were hoisted by our own petard, we were well and truly sunk.

IV. Capitulation And Recapitulation

I have no memory of swooning, but I will never forget recovering consciousness at the top of that improbable tower. My self-disgust at passing out like the simpering heroine of dime-novel cliché was allayed by the realisation that both Kong and the professor were also recovering from fainting spells. I concluded fuzzily that we had all been drugged. Our guns were gone, but someone had had sufficient decency to leave me with my handbag. Then I managed to focus on my surroundings and was greeted by the nauseating sight of a nearly naked Monty Monk wearing what looked like a giant turban and holding hands with similarly attired stilt-men.

"Quisling quack-quack blancmange," Monty announced.

"Toad snipe, toad snipe!" one of the Moon-men snapped, and Monty adjusted his strange headgear.

"Ah, hello? Oh yes, much better! Evening all!"

"What in the blue blazes is going on, dear boy?" the professor demanded. "What have these lanky fiends done to you?"

Monty laughed with a peculiarly girlish giggle. "I'm in the club! I've become a member of the lunar élite." We looked at him as if he had lost the last of the few wits that God had given him. "The tall chaps are just servants around here, you see – it's the floaty fellows on our heads who are *la crème de la crème* around here." The strange hats did indeed look like swollen brains, and I realised with a shock that the clouds we had seen scudding towards the tower had actually been these curious lumps of grey matter.

"Long, long ago," Monty went on, "before their ancestors came down from the stars and colonised the interior of the Moon, they were all the same. Then evolution took over. The menials who did the work stayed on the ground, growing ever longer legs to get around the swamps, while the nobility simply evolved into a more gaseous form of lighter-than-air being that could float free and enjoy the high life. Nowadays, the élite either sun themselves around the lodestone that holds the air in and lights up the place, or pop down, sit on people's heads and tell their minions what do. It's absolutely super! They want me to be part of it – and you too –"

"Now, Monty," I said, "no one ever pretended that you were the sharpest blade in the shaving kit, but presumably, since you haven't yet learned to fly, this would mean that they want you to be one of their slaves too."

"Would it?" Monty asked before adjusting the brain-beast squatting on his head, as if he was tuning the cat's whisker of a wireless set. "Oh, right, yes – it would."

"Beatle wig, sandwich board, fondue," one of the stilt-men ordered sternly while pointing at the three of us with a sucker-tipped finger. We were hauled to our feet and dragged towards a ledge like a gangplank at the edge of the tower. Three floating brains drifted towards us with menacing intent, their eyestalks and vestigial limbs wriggling greedily.

"Montgomery Montgolfier Monk, you are a disgrace to your country and the Crown!" Professor MacGuffin said with disgust. "You may be quite content to wander about naked as the day you were born wearing a power-crazed tea-cosy on your head, but I, sir, am certainly *not* of that kidney!" The professor struggled, but even under the lesser lunar gravity, he could not shake off his captors. "I am prepared to fight the mesmeric might of these malevolent mentalists with my own will, but spare the lesser fortitude of the woman and my servant –"

Kong turned his placid and inscrutable face to me, and whispered a few words of comfort: "Madam, as I believe Confucius himself once said, 'Sod this for a game of soldiers!'"

He moved with startling grace, catching his captors off balance and flinging them bodily into the guards holding me. Then the Chinaman's hands and feet moved with uncanny speed in the reduced gravity, chopping and kicking this way and that. The spindly guards were sent flying and we were free for a moment, but more of the puppet-like stilt-men were already charging up the stairs to seize us.

"Miss Underhill," Kong cried, even as he was brought down and gagged, "your cigarette lighter –"

It seemed odd that any man should suggest that a woman should commit the social *faux pas* of smoking outside, even at a time like this. However, as one of the floating monsters reared above me, I guessed what he meant. If the things were lighter than air, then they had to contain pockets of gas like a Zeppelin – gas that was probably combustible.

In a trice, I pulled my lighter from my bag and struck the flint. The brain-beast veered, but I tickled its underside with the naked flame.

There was ghastly, flatulent bang and the ugly lump of grey matter shot off like a skyrocket before exploding messily in mid-air. Everyone else froze for a moment. I advanced on the other creatures, all perched like substandard millinery on the stilt-men's heads, and the rout began.

The humid and watery environment of the lunar interior had meant that fire, the Achilles' heel of the floating dictators, had never troubled them before. Once some of the stilt-men had been released from their mental bondage, their minds soon cleared, and they helped us to liberate more of their kind. All-out revolution was in progress around the tower before long. Freedom spread – and I choose my words with care – like wildfire. The brain-beasts knew they were toast and fled for the skies, floating dejectedly away from the lands they had ruled so poorly.

We returned to our launch escorted by a host of joyful stilt-men.

"Parsnip! Parsnip!" they cried gratefully as we cast off, but the comment was lost on us. We tried to be polite by randomly shouting the names of other root vegetables back at them.

We returned to the Omniscope portal uneventfully, and were pleasantly surprised to re-enter the world we knew in time for breakfast.

V. Coda In Codicil

"So you see, I *was* on the Moon," Ursula Underhill concluded with a twinkle in her eye.

I stared at her, quite lost for words. "Oh, don't concern yourself, young man, I didn't expect you to believe me. Now, could you take my bag and escort me to my room? I am weary and must retire."

As I took Ursula by the arm and helped her to the elevator, I finally found my voice.

"Why did you never tell anyone before?"

"Well, that was the first thing Monty did. They put him in the booby hatch for a couple of years before he learnt to keep his trap shut."

"What about the professor?"

"Oh, he wanted to hush it all up. I had worked out that Kong was responsible for most of the actual work, and the old fool was ashamed that he had taken credit for another man's work – a Chinaman's creation at that. The 'professor' title was also a sore point. I don't believe he'd ever attended a university, let alone taught at one…"

"And the redoubtable Kong?"

"Well, I don't know much about the martial arts, but I can assure you that he was very accomplished at the marital ones. We were wed the following spring, you see."

We reached her room and I helped her to a cushioned chair. Ursula asked me to open her bag and place its contents on the dressing table.

"A gift from my late husband," she told me.

I found a curious box, not unlike a manual typewriter, with brass controls and some kind of projector.

"I'm so old, my dear," she said sadly. "My bones are brittle and all my friends have gone. I'm not long for this world, you know."

"It's been an honour," I said, and left her to her thoughts.

Then a strange thing happened in the hallway. I heard a pop, saw a purple flash, and then someone or something clearly said, "Semolina trouser press."

Ursula Underhill's door swung open and, concerned, I went back in, but there was no one there and the curious gift from Kong had gone too. Outside the window, a full moon hung over the New York skyline.

I bowed politely in its direction, saying, "Parsnip, parsnip," before I left the room again and gently closed the door.

Andrew J. Wilson is an Edinburgh-based writer, editor and spoken-word performer. Recent work has appeared in: *Professor Challenger: New Worlds, Lost Places; Dystopia Utopia Short Stories; Umbrellas of Edinburgh; and Scotia Extremis.* With Neil Williamson, he co-edited the award-nominated anthology *Nova Scotia: New Scottish Speculative Fiction.*

46 Candlemaker Row
Edinburgh
EH1 2QE

0131 226 6266
www.transreal.co.uk
enquiries@transreal.co.uk
@transrealshop

Scotland's best selection of new science
fiction and fantasy books and a large
range of art books.

*Find us on Candlemaker Row, just down from
Greyfriars Bobby.*

Model Organisms

Caroline Grebbell

I **have never considered** a companion – is that the word? – an organism to interact with. It has been such a lengthy duration and I was unaware of the existence of your kind – the existence of any of this – until relocated from Japeng Aquatic. Yes, the temperature is higher in Phototropi, but still humid. Throughout the last dyau-sequence I have been feeling my mass, which is new to me, and it weighs heavy. I am euryhaline but the first of mine to invert to terra. For genera I have laid immersed within the covalent bonds of Aquatic. Cold sodium chloride, then warmer habitats free of halite. Now I advance bipedally, neither one thing or the other. My new bones are durable. Microgravity activates the osteoclasts; they are fluorescent, quite mesmeric I once overheard, although I have never seen them myself as my retinas become

weakened. You will view me as colourless, my skin is dehydrated.

I was a model organism, as you were Thaliana. There for the determination of genes, toxicology, transgenic and haploid embryonic stem cells. I was brought here to help them learn. To assist them. That's what I believed. That's what they told me. I was numerous at first but have evolved to one. To this. I realise you are aware of all I say, Thaliana, I tell you each time we converse. I apologise, it is all I know, it is all that is left for me to say but to say nothing for want of something new is further suffering.

When did this split appear, this chasm between spirit and physical worlds? How can a spirit exist four-hundred kilometers above its planet drowned? Anima? Your kind will remember her.

I have been here the longest of durations. I have spawned brood but they are from the other, the Oryzias, the Meduka. They shifted me, stretched me, twisted my form. They have lost me and now I am losing you. Six dyau-sequence is too short a duration for you to flourish. I was permitted to observe you Thaliana, you are exemplary. You may indeed be mesmeric. The permission was a distraction I know, to push reasoning from my solitude. But solitude is not the focus of my reasoning. I exist more humanoid than Oryzias now, my scales have levelled, my surface lanulose, spermatozoa multiplies in my ovaries. I am neither one thing nor the other. From seed to germination I have tended you Thaliana. You flowered then to seed once more and now you are dying. To be pulled apart. Sectioned and evaluated. I too will be recalled for dissection but I am unknowing as to when. Unknowing as to what I will become. They have left me like this. My life ends and I do not know what I am.

And now we are to be separated. I am scared. I have seen so little. The True Aquatic was my home and then my jailer. I am lonely. We co-exist beneath the electro-rad of this artificial sunne. I fail to find even the remnants of a shadow in this habitat.

Should we ever wonder how it resulted in this, us and not the others, what did we show over them? Nothing perhaps. Nothing other than being plucked from the ether.

Do you live your memories? Ancient and distant but beyond my reach, they are duration-worn and strange, as if perhaps not my belonging at all. Perhaps they bind to the being I was before me or link to the me I am to become. An untroubled duration has been the one spent with you. And now you are dying. Your gestation is over, your span, and I am to be left alone. My bones are strong but my muscles grow stiff and rigid. I am lonely, Thaliana. I am atrophied and dying and they will watch me shrink and wither and turn their backs to continue their search. I am scared, Thaliana. Perhaps I will block my gills with your flowers and we can travel together.

Caroline Grebbell is a Belfast born European who lives between Scotland and France. She is collaborating on a graphic novel script and writing more Sci-Fi. *Model Organisms* was longlisted for the BSFA Short Fiction Award. Twitter: @Grebbell web: www.carolinegrebbell.co.uk

Edinburgh Masks

Adam Roberts

Art: Siobhan McDonald

His Iago was no good. Not that the audience seemed to have noticed. Or perhaps they noticed but didn't care. Harringay cared, of course, and now Harringay was sitting beside him in the Theatre Royal's bijou dressing room extirpating his negro face with cold cream and a rag. "Did you eat, old boy?" Foresman tried. "We could pick up a crumb in the King's Charger."

"I ate before the performance," said Harringay, coldly. "And of course Mrs Harringay is expecting me."

"Of course."

As Harringay rose, Foresman blurted: "I'll perk up the evil, tomorrow, old chap, you know." Harringay, walking out, did not reply.

"And a good evening to *you*, sir," Foresman said, mournfully, to his reflection in the dressing-room mirror. "And to *you* sir a very good evening."

At the stage door the porter clasped Foresman's elbow, and then disappeared into his nook. Foresman waited as patiently as he was able, patience not really being his *forte*. The whole of Edinburgh was hissing him softly, just on the far side of the exit door. The whole city. He called through to the little back room: "Macbrie, did Mr Hellespont leave a note concerning the casting of *A Way To Pay Old Debts*?"

"Not at all, sir," came Macbrie's voice.

"*The Ragpicker of Paris*? He assuredly mentioned a role in *The Ragpicker of Paris* last week."

"Not that, sir."

"He may have left a note."

Macbrie re-emerged, holding a wrapped object the size of a small guitar. "No note, sir, though Mr Hellespont did call, left flowers for Miss Gertie."

"And that?"

"This, sir."

"And that's for me?"

"Yes, sir," said Macbrie, holding the thing out. "I've wrapped it in oilcloth against the rain, but will be obliged when you return the cloth, coming in for tomorrow's performance."

Foresman almost groaned at the thought of going through the whole sorry charade again tomorrow. *For when my outward action doth demonstrate The native act and figure of my heart* – oh, he could weep. Veritably weep! "What is it?"

"Masks," said Macbrie.

"Masks?"

"Such a pair of smiling, and also the frowning, masks," said Macbrie, "as signify the theatrical arts, sir."

"I don't understand," said Foresman. "Are you sure they're for me?"

"Individual most particular, directed them to you."

"I don't understand," said Foreman, rubbing his tired eyes. "Are they a gift?"

"Will be appreciative," muttered Macbrie, "upon the return of the oilcloth on the occasion of you coming in tomorrow, sir."

Foresman took the parcel, turned up his collar, and stepped through the stage door into the rain outside. The night sky all geese, the universe mocking his Iago, as he picked his way up the murk of Leith Way to his digs. It took three separate bouts of knocking before Mrs McHoakham opened her door, and he was thoroughly wet by the time he got to his room. He lit a candle. There was but half a shovelful of coal left. He had no desire to haggle with Mrs McHoakham about obtaining more, not so late in the night. Still: he could hardly sit there, shivering wet in the cold. He made what small fire he could in the grate, scraped off his wet clothes and wrapped a blanket about his shoulders. There was a kneecap-sized bit of bread left, and some cheese, hard, and he ate these, and washed it all down with whisky – to warm himself, he said, rather than because he felt maudlin.

He took a look at the masks.

They were, as the porter had said, the masks of comedy and tragedy, carved in dark wood – ebony, perhaps – and linked together with a bar at the back. For display, presumably. There was a curious aspect to their design, for they were carved in such a way as they retained their expressions when inverted. This tromp l'oeil design intrigued Foresman. The creased brow on Tragedy became its woestruck mouth when the pair were turned about, and the laughing raised brows of Comedy performed the same function for that face's smiling lips. It was a gimmick of course, but quite a cunning one. But who had gifted it to him? He ought to have pressed Mcbrie on the provenance of the thing. Was it Hellespont? If it was Hellespont, then might it be the wily old Greek's way of dismissing him from the life of an actor? But that would be a strange way of giving notice. They might be valuable. They were certainly curious. Perhaps he could pawn them?

His Iago had been bad tonight.

Foresman leaned the double mask against the wainscot beside the fireplace and looked down upon the thing. He sipped a little more whisky. From time to time he reached down and turned the connected faces turvy-topsy, and then he looked at them some more. The fire cracked one of its coals with a gunshot sound, and it was as if the mask coughed. When it began to speak he was almost not surprised.

"Frederick Albert Foresman," said the left hand mask – Tragedy. Its voice was bright, for so mournful a face.

"Moses and Mary!" exclaimed the actor.

"Sitting in your chair," said the mask, "squinting and scowling at me."

"I am drunk," said Foresman in a loud voice, as if trying to persuade himself. "Or *you* are possessed by a devil."

"A," agreed the mask, "or *the*, and you're not so *very* drunk." Its mouth opened and closed with no splintering of the liquorish-coloured wood. It flowed and folded exactly like skin. The hollowed-out eyes narrowed, and widened. There was something indescribably unnerving about it.

"No, no," said Foresman. "I've no desire to talk to the devil." A twist of the old, old fear, the oldest in fact, of human anxiety in the face of the rivalry of brute nature against human hope, swelled in his abdomen. On a whim he reached down and turned the double-mask about, as if that would silence it. It still spoke, but now it was the right-hand mask, grinning at the cosmic hilarity of it all, out of which the words came.

"Your whole life has been dedicated to Thespis," said the mask, smilingly. "You have only ever wanted to be a great actor. And yet your acting is mediocre!"

Foresman reached down and picked up the linked masks, with a half-formed idea of tossing them on the fire. It was burning low now, the meagre supply of coals consuming themselves.

"Stay your hand," said the mask. "I want to make you an offer – a genuine offer. You lack inspirations for your craft, and I can supply those."

Foresman peered closely at the artefact. Under his fingers it was unimpeachably wood, carved and solid. And yet the mouth moved, and the wood, hard to the touch, had the fluidity of flesh. "At the cost of my soul, I suppose?"

"A bargain must be reciprocal to be a bargain, of course."

"Oh I am drunk," said Foresman. "Drunk on Scottish whisky! Drunk on despair!"

"And what good is your soul to you," the mask asked, "in such a predicament?"

"Do you think I want to go to perdition simply for the acting of a tolerable Iago before a crowd of Scotsmen munching oranges and cracking nuts?"

"One performance, only?" the mask said. "No. That would be a cheap of me, insulting cheap. I am more generous than that. I offer you seven."

"Seven performances?"

"Complete runs, naturally. If you contract for a twelvemonth as Volpone, then that whole twelvemonth shall be one seventh of my bargain. Seven! The greatest performances in the history of theatre, to be the talk of ages to come wherever the drama is discussed. Seven indubitable masterpiece performances, all for a Chelsea actor's soul. It's a bargain?"

Perhaps Foresman was not so assiduous about attending church as he ought to be, but that did not mean he had forgotten all his Sunday School teaching. The thought came to him, then, of his long-suffering mother, and her cough like a shovel of gravel being tuned over in her chest, the cough that had increased in frequency from a few times an hour to a few times a minute, and which had gained resonance and penetration as it began spotting her white handkerchiefs red. Some of her devotion to God and goodness had rubbed off even on father, even though it mostly manifested in him as superstition. How could a son resist it? Throw the demonic toy in the flames, before the flames died away entirely – for if the fire died out, he'd be stuck with its yammering all through the night.

Foresman drew it back to toss the thing in. "Seven," said the mask, again.

And he hesitated.

He put the mask back in his lap, and picked up his whisky tumbler. And this was the thought going through his mind: if I am contracted, on pain of losing my eternal soul, to seven performances, and I only give six, then I cheat the devil of his bargain, and make a mighty reputation for myself at the same time. This thought woke something like childish delight inside him, at his own cunning. Why, he told himself, I could do *five* great performances, and retire, with two in hand, to be on the safe side! Or I could even – for who is to say I won't? – I could even agree to this bargain, return to the Royal tomorrow and triumph as Iago and *then* walk away! Wouldn't it be worth it, to see the expression on Harringay's black-painted face? To make Hellespont come crawling back to me with offers of Hamlet and Oedipus and Richard III?

"How would I accede to this bargain you are offering?" he asked.

"Say the word," said the mask, turned about now to tragedy. "Say *yes* and it will be sealed."

"And you will hold to your part of it?"

"Such things are governed by a power beyond mine to suborn," said the mask. "You can trust that I will hold to it, however much I might wish to break it."

"Yes," said Foresman, and threw the mask in the fire.

The wood took a while to catch, and for several minutes it only smoked an oily-looking black smoke that went straight up the flue. Foresman wondered if the thing was going to scream in pain, or in betrayal, but the faces were fixed now, and silent, and soon enough the flames caught at the wood and the little room became, for a short while at any rate, quite cosy and warm. Foresman finished his whisky, and then betook himself to bed, and he slept a deep sleep, and woke in the morning feeling unsure whether the whole thing had been a waking dream, or even, conceivably, a dreaming dream.

Except that there were fragments of charred wood in the grate. And here was Mcbrie's oilcloth, folded and ready to be returned.

He felt just the same in the daylight as he had done the previous day, and in all the days before that one, so he decided that the previous night had been nothing more than hallucination. The first intimation he had that things were different was when he stepped onto the stage for the matinee, striding alongside Barnaby's foppish Roderigo. His first word, a *sblood*, got lost somewhere in a strange little hiccough of the diaphragm, but then

If ever I did dream of such a matter,
Abhor me

came out with a strange force. And all through the first act he could feel something new in his performance, a magnetic quality that held the audience still and rapt. By the time of the thus do I ever make my fool my purse monologue, it was manifest that something special was occurring in the stage. Foresman could see the whole company who were not on stage gathered in both wings to watch the performance, which was unprecedented. At the play's end the auditorium was filled with a thunderstorm of applause, with hootings and bravos, and when the cast took their bows he – Freddie Foresman, of Oakley Street London – received a greater volume of accolade even than Harringay. That didn't make the old boy happy, of course. You could see that because he put on a smiling face, and congratulated Foresman a little too heartily, and shook his hand with a touch too much vigour. But the rest of the cast, and all the stage hands, crowded round him, and they took him off to a local tavern and treated him to beer. "Did you see Harry's hangdog face?" laughed Barnaby.

"How he hates to be upstaged!" "He's waiting to see if you can replicate that marvel in the first evening show," was Slattery's opinion. "If you do, old boy, oh he'll be furious."

And so it proved. Foresman was even more electric in the evening show. One could almost hear Harringay grinding his teeth as he shook his hand goodnight.

The following day the rumour was that Harringay and Hellespont had had a falling out. The old Greek had heard something was up and taken the rare step of attending the evening performance, said Slattery. Harringay wanted Foresman dismissed from the company, and Hellespont wasn't having any of that, so they two had had Words. It did nothing to improve Harringay's Moor, which only made Foresman's Iago shine the brighter. By the end of the week there were notices in the paper, and tickets for the remainder of the run were sold out. Unprecedented! And everybody knew it had nothing to do with Harringay's creaky old *Let me not name it to you, you chaste stars*. You could hear the collective indrawn breath of the audience as Foresman delivered *I hate the Moor*. It was like a steam whistle.

Hellespont was, suddenly, all over him; treating him to food, arranging for superior digs closer to the theatre, and – *mirabile!* – offering him leads. Leads! "Don't eh-want to eh-waste you, my boy," he said, confidentially, "in *Ragpicker*. Trash, that play. Trash. Eh-we need a classic to eh-show you off, like fine jewel in eh-gold.

Hamlet! It is too common a mistake," he pronounced, slapping his meaty palm on the table, "that eh-Hamlet is cast too *old*. Eh-fifty, sixty, seventy, eh-absurd! Hamlet is eh-young man's role."

It was the first Foresman had heard of any *Hamlet* run. "Here, in Edinburgh?"

"London!" howled Hellespont, positively howled, and clapped for more wine to be brought over.

It was all a whirl, and Foresman was carried along with it. It was not until the Saturday of the penultimate week that any thought as to consequences rose up in his brain. It was a chance comment, after yet another storming performance, and Harringay had petulantly left the stage whilst the rest were still taking their bows, and all but he had repaired to the King's Charger for post-play drinks. It was here that Miss Gertie – very attentive to him, now, when before she hadn't so much as deigned to notice him in the hallway – made a passing comment about how Freddie must have struck a deal with an old Highland witch to transform his acting so. That was too close to the bone to be comfortable. Slattery mocked her for not being able to distinguish her Highlands and her Lowlands and she retorted that the whole Land of Scots should split their differences and settle upon a Middle-Height-lands. Foresman laughed and quaffed and staggered back to his spacious hotel room, where, without him having to ask, a boy was sent up by Management to light the fire for him. Still the thought chewed at the edges of his mind. *Had* he struck a deal?

He didn't have to consider the question. He knew he had.

He consoled himself with the thought that he had contracted for seven famous performances, and had performed but the one. Six in hand! He could Hamlet himself to fame in London, and take a free choice of a follow up role, and then retire – retiring at twenty-six would only cement his reputation as the greatest of the great, surely. And no longer-term harm would be done. He resolved this with himself, and went so far as foolishly to shake his own hand on it, in front of a mirror, grinning like an idiot, before filling the chamber pot and going to bed. But his night was not peaceful, and dark dreams kept trembling him to the lip of wakefulness before sinking him back down again. In the morning, to the sound of church bells, he washed quickly and dressed perfunctorily and scurried along to a granite church on Lothian road that had a spire like a poignard – chosen only because it was the closest. Here he took a seat at the back, and endured an interminable sermon, and sang hymns where he wasn't sure of the Scots melody, and prayed when everybody prayed. Afterwards, strolling in the Sunday sunlight, he felt better. He had not, he decided, cut himself off irrevocably from the mercy and the love of God. The church doors were always open to him.

For the time being, at any rate, his inner voice whispered.

For the time being.

Othello came to the end of its run, and Harringay became uncharacteristically drunken at the after-gathering, and made a scene (appropriate for an actor, that, when you came to think of it) publicly accusing Foresman of spying on him in order to steal his (Harringay's) acting tricks and shifts and so pass himself off as a new Edmund Kean in side-whiskers. He, Harringay, *he* had performed at a private show for Princess Alexandra! Prince Christian of Denmark himself had commended him, after he (Harringay) had performed Alceste the Misanthrope *in the original French*, mark you! Then Harringay sat down, and doubled over, and was sick onto his own shins and shoes, and Hellespont had to take him home. Foresman had never felt so elated. If ever his spirits sagged, even for a moment, he reminded himself inwardly that he had six performances in hand – even if he only used a couple of them, he had ample opportunity to establish his reputation as the greatest actor of his epoch. Of all time!

And so he came down to London and began rehearsals for *Hamlet,* and even in the poky Chancery Lane rooms Hellespont had hired for the read-throughs the magic was palpable. The other players noted it. People treated him with a new respect. The show opened at the Aquarium in Wesminster, recently renamed the Imperial Theatre. Never have reviews so universally dithyrambic appeared in the national press! Never has word-of-mouth spread so quickly! *The Times* called Foresman's the definitive Hamlet of the age. Audiences gasped and sighed at his monologues, and wept at his death. He received letters by the satchel-ful, praising, exhorting, begging for personal meetings. Grown men wrote to say that watching him play had convinced them to reform their lives. Women offered themselves in marriage.

The run made Foresman relatively little money, since wily Hellespont kept him on a flat fee rather than cutting him a percentage. Beforehand the fee had seemed to the young actor princely, but by the end of the run he understood that he had been swindled. Still he had four more charmed performances in hand, retaining the buffer-zone of the seventh unutilised, so there was no need to scrape by. He was firm with Hellespont: no more sharp practice, or he would take himself off to another manager who would treat him better. The Greek made convincing atonement, and together they drew up plans for a lavish production of Taylor's *Ticket-of-Leave Man*, with Foresman as Brierly, and Henry Gartside Neville, no less, as Hawksmoor. The deal was a fifty-fifty split of all profits, with Neville paid out of Hellespont's share. The play opened at the Gaiety, on the Strand, and ran for two years.

It made Foresman rich, which had been the idea. It added to his glory, too. Reviewers declared that his performance translated a creaky old melodrama into high art – never before, said Sir Taylor Brindsley in the *London Gazette*, had the pathos, humanity and dignity of Brierly's situation come home to him with such force. Though the groundlings might still applaud and weep as the plot turned its surprises round and about, the more discerning audience member would see, for the first time, that this was a play capable of interrogating the randomness of chance in human affairs, the power of human endurance and the redemptive power of love.

Swept up by his own powers, Foresman proposed marriage to his sweetheart, beautiful young Marie Delaroche. The ceremony was covered in all the society papers. He bought a Mayfair townhouse, retained three servants and a cook, and settled into his comfortable life.

Long before the run came to an end, Foresman was besieged by theatrical agents propositioning him. His morning mail was equal parts letter from adoring members of the public, and proposals of new productions. Hellespont begged him to continue, but Foresman was wealthy enough now, and shook his head. At this Hellespont begged to be taken on as Foresman's agent, and to this, to save himself the pettifogging bother of managing himself, or finding another agent for the position, Foresman agreed.

He had three charmed performances in hand, and decided to use only one more of them: for he did not want future histories of the Victorian stage to record that his last rôle on stage had been in a crowd-pleaser like Ticket-of-Leave Man. So he contracted to perform as Pentheus, in a new translation of Euripides Bacchae by a young Irishman called Wilde. Fanny Kemble was persuaded to play Agave, and the play was an immediate critical hit. Foresman had insisted upon an open-ended run, for he had resolved with himself that this would be his swan song, and there was no urgency about such a thing. Critics loved it, of course. He himself could feel the power he exuded upon the stage – audiences gasped and clutched their hands to their chest. Yet the play was not so successful, financially, as the Ticket of Leave man. It was a bald truth: no matter how good he was in the part, Greek Tragedy was too refined and high a taste for the average London theatre-goer, and the lavishness of the production made it harder than it would otherwise have been to turn a profit. Foresman blamed himself: it had been pride, and the thought that this would be his last show, that had prompted him to spare no expense, and when he called an end to the run, the house two thirds empty for most performances, it was to discover that the entire exercise, so far from being financially advantageous, had cost him somewhere near £1000.

That was provoking, of course. He had his clippings book, and the reviews were as adoring as ever; although perhaps even there a sense was creeping into the critics' prose that wonders and splendour were routine for an actor such as he. That was the very least that might be expected. They were, he complained to Marie, taking him for granted. Him! Marie bowed her head and murmured agreement.

Still – Iago, Hamlet, Briers and Pentheus, out of the seven, still left him two in hand and one to be left over. He could afford to rescue his financial situation with another leading role, and *then* retire – move into management, to directing other players, writing his memoirs, teaching acting at ten guineas an hour. There were many possibilities. So he played Mathias, in a revival of *The Bells*; and the papers agreed with impressive unanimity that he had laid the ghost even of Henry Irving's celebrated performance. He cleared more than £4000 after two years and took Marie on a Continental tour by way of celebration.

Now was the time to call it a day. There was no question about that. Foresman invested a sum of money in a school for actors, and for a while was content. Marie suffered two miscarriages in consecutive years, the second of which put her life in danger for weeks; and afterwards he took a house in the south of France for the winter to help her convalesce. They liked it down there so much they stayed through the following year, and saw in the new century on the Continent. When Foresman returned to London it was to discover that his acting school had so far failed to prosper in his absence as to have become a dead loss. His personal tuition drew some students, but the school as a whole was failing, losing money quarter after quarter, and in 1902 there was nothing to do but close it. It was provoking, but there you go.

A new generation of actors were being celebrated on the London stage, some of them (provokingly enough) in terms that echoed the praise Foresman had enjoyed in his day. It dawned on him slowly that he was yesterday's man. His name was mentioned with respect, but his fame was a historical curio rather than a living fact. He tried to accept this, and, hiring an amanuensis, devoted a summer to writing his life story. He did not mention the Edinburgh masks, of course. A folk tale, and such an implausible one, could only be harmful to his reputation. Quite apart from anything else, he did not want people crediting his electrifying dramatic performances to anything other than his genius as an actor. The book did moderately well. Reviews were respectful rather than enthusiastic. Sales were modest. It didn't matter. He had never wanted to be an author.

And anyway. Did he really believe that the *masks* were what underwrote his success? Poor, tired and a little drunk, a mere speculative vision in an Edinburgh bedsit. He didn't even know whom had gifted him the masks – when he had asked, the porter at the theatre had not recalled.

There were whole hours – stretches of continuous time, in the brightness of daylight – when he almost convinced himself that the whole of that business was just a quirk of his youth. A mere fancy. But then twilight would soak into the world, and his gaslights would shine their light, and clouds of birds would mesh with the trees that lined the road and settle for the night, and the simple truth of his bargain reverted to his mind.

He had made the deal. He had said 'yes'.

He wished he had been more acute when it came to striking the bargain. He could, for instance, have insisted upon the right to choose when he would act magnificently, and so intersperse his grand performances with a number of mediocre ones. But that possibility was not open to him now. Marie's health improved a little, but he himself suffered badly from gout. He took to walking with a stick.

A writer came to interview him for a book, *Great Actors of the Nineteenth-Century*. "And might I ask, sir, why you elected to retire from the stage?"

"It was," Foresman lied, smoothing his moustache between finger and thumb, "so as to be better placed to care for my wife."

Marie was sick again, certainly, although she required little by way of care, for she spent most of her time in bed. Her lungs got worse, and then stabilised, and then worsened again. Foresman took a house in Cannes, overlooking a sea as blue as Marie's own eyes. Hers was a slow decline, but inexorable; and two years in France all but drained Foresman's funds. Besides which, Marie was homesick for England. So he sold his Mayfair house and bought a small place in the countryside, near Bagshot. He became a regular communicant at All Saints Church, and prayed to God every night before going to bed, like an earnest schoolboy. He had not gone beyond the pale – he knew it, in his heart, his whole spirit told him. Seven great performances the devil had told him, and he had given the world five, five towering acting roles that transformed people's lives. He had done it, and cheated the devil of his bargain. It was the glory of God in the end, that was what mattered.

But his life felt thin. He was content, or more-or-less content, but there was a *thinness* in the days. Life was less vivid nowadays. Perhaps all men felt this, as they grew older. Foresman strode up and down Berkshire lanes in the summer sun, cutting down the tall dandelions with his walking stick as if he were decapitating the enemy. Something missing, some infant voice echoing in his mind, *I want, I want.*

Marie grew more sick. The medical bills combined with Foresman's habitual financial improvidence to push him into debt. It wasn't the debt that sent him back to the stage, though. Or it wasn't only the debt. He was finding it hard to live as a once-was, a historical footnote. He was only in his fifties! Some of the greatest actors had done their best work at his age. And he had two performances in hand before he reached the seven. He could spare one more.

Hellespont was dead, now, but there were other theatrical agents only too happy to arrange a return of the Great Foresman to the London stage. He chose *Macbeth*, a play, he felt sure, that would draw an audience. It was a success, too: a year's run booked-in, remarkable notices, audiences rapt. And it brought something back into Foresman's life the thing that he had not been able to put a name to – it was power, the power to hold the crowd's attention, to manipulate their emotions, to reach into their hearts and wrench the tender muscle.

His Macbeth was a triumph, no question. But the play *Macbeth* lived up to its malign reputation. Stuttercock, playing Banquo, broke his ankle. Duncan had a stroke. A man died of a heart attack in row seven – died in Act One, but wasn't discovered dead until Act Four when his companion finally noticed and began shrieking and wailing. The set caught on fire, although the blaze was contained. A motor truck crashed into the foyer, causing two concussions and a shattered collar bone amongst the exiting crowd. Rumour wandered London wearing his coat of many tongues, and people stayed away. People came to the box office to return their tickets and made a fuss when they did not receive a full refund.

Foresman was in his dressing room, having delivered an electrifying performance to a quarter-full auditorium, when the news was delivered to him that Marie had died. They had known earlier, but hadn't wanted to put him off his stride for the evening show.

He nodded. Of course.

He turned down the offer of a cab and walked his way back to his hotel through the narrow canyons of London's highways. Down to the Thames to rest his eyes and cool his head, watching the variegated lights upon the river. Through the arches of Waterloo Bridge a hundred points of light, white, and orange, and red, marked the sweep of the Embankment, and above its parapet rose the towers of Westminster, a dead grey block against the starlight. The black river went by with only a rare ripple breaking its silence, passing over its oiled surface like a snake to disturb the reflections of the lights.

He'd been a fool, he saw. It came to him with shattering certainty. His pride had brought him to the very brink – six performances of the seven the Devil had promised him, and though they *were* great, they mattered no more than and flotsam sweeping down the river in the nighttime. In two decades he would be dead, and in fifty years he would be a footnote in a dusty academic history of the theatre that nobody read, and in a thousand years London itself would be mere ruins. If H G Wells was to be believed, in a hundred thousand years there would not be such creatures as homo sapiens anywhere upon the face of the globe – and yet all that time would pass like an eyeblink for God in his citadel of eternity.

Why had he taken such an absurd risk? Pride, only pride. Had he truly believed that his prancing about on stage in any way magnified the glory of God? Attempting a cheat the Prince of Darkness of his bargain, all the while accruing worldly glory and fame and money for himself? His folly was laid bare to him. It was all pride, absurd pride, dangerous and sinful pride.

There, in the open air beside the great river, Foresman went onto his knees and prayed to God.

The next day he arranged for the cancellation of the run. His manager put up some small objection, but Foresman could see he was secretly relieved. The end was reported on page 3 of *Variety*, and adverts were taken out at the back of the respectable dailies offering refunds to advance ticket holders. Foresman returned to his Bagshot house, hollow and echoing without Marie. He ought to have been with her when she passed. That fact brought tears to his eyes.

He went into mourning, and was more assiduous in his church attendance, and prayed ever more lengthily each night. But he could at least take comfort from one thought: though he had come to the brink, he had not stepped over the lip. He had a vision of his own future – brooding over the one great performance that still left in him, but which could only be purchased at the cost of his soul. He saw himself waiting through all the long years of the rest of his life, eating up his own heart in bitterness, obsessing over it, until finally he could take it no longer. Finally he would crack. But of *course* he would crack, his mind worrying away at the thought of it like a tongue probing a raging tooth – he *would* fall, and walk the boards again as Agamemnon or Sir Peter Teazle or Tartuffe, to applause and admiration and his own eternal damnation. Like a man addicted to some terrible opium, he would be unable to resist.

How close it had been! But though the Devil was strong, God was stronger. Foresman turned his back on the theatrical world, repudiated it utterly. The nation was on the brink of war with Germany, and though too old to serve himself, he helped where he could to raise volunteers from the Sunningdale and Ascot parishes. He sold his house and bought a smaller one in the village of Bracknell, and resolved to live modestly.

He thought about it more and more, and the conclusion was inevitable. It could not be shirked. It was *theatre itself* that was the problem. The Puritans had been right to ban it! How could it be anything other than a snare of pride, parading yourself before your fellow sinners puffed up in your vanity? Pretending to be someone other than who you were – that is, *lying*. For what else is acting, in plain language, but the performance of a lie? Foresman had spent decades in that world, and had experienced it at every level, and he *knew*. Not for nothing was *actress* practically a synonym for *prostitute*. Theatre was a gutter art for a gutter age.

He saw then, with a clarity that felt like visionary revelation, what the whole business with the masks had been about. The ways of God are sometimes winding, but they bring the true soul eventually about to redemption – for the Devil *had* tempted him, and he had *dallied* with the Devil, thinking to fool him, but had only sunk himself deeper and deeper into pride and misery and spiritual danger. And at the last minute, with only one performance standing between himself and the hot pit of hell, divine grace had touched him.

He arranged to speak with the vicar at All Saints in Ascot – a worthy man called Oldfield, honestly bald of head and bristly of chin, with a courteous manner. "Reverend," Foresman told him, "I have been reflecting on my days as an actor."

"As," Oldfield said, ingratiatingly, "one of the greatest of actors."

"That's it exactly," said Foresman. "I have thought about this a good deal, and prayed, and it is clear to me now that all that," he gestured behind him with his hand, "was – sin."

"Come now, my dear Foresman," said the vicar. "This is no Catholic chapel. Are you really coming to me for confession?"

"I am speaking less of myself, although of course I know I am a sinner. But I mean the stage itself. The theatre! The Puritans were right to ban it. It is deceit and pride – it is the very performance of deceit and pride. It is the devil's delight. You don't ever," he added, "read of Jesus attending a play, in the New Testament, do you? Or the apostles? They go all over Greece, and write their letters from Corinth and so on. That's where theatre began, Pagan Greece, but the apostles will have nothing to do with any of that." This had seemed to him, when it had occurred to him, sitting alone in his front room, a very powerful and persuasive point, but now that he spoke it aloud to the Reverend it struck him as banal. Oldfield appeared to agree.

"Come now," the vicar said, "That Jesus never smoked a cigar, or wore patent leather boots, doesn't mean that boots and smokes are damned. Some theatre *is* low and corruptive of morals, of course. But there's surely nothing intrinsically wicked about the theatre. Why, think of the Mysteries! Or schoolchildren performing a Nativity Play! That's not…" Oldfield seemed to lose his thread. "I mean, you wouldn't say *that* was… ahem. Hem hem!"

Foresman nodded gravely. "I'm sure you are correct. I daresay I am – I might say, mine is an overreaction." He thought about telling Oldfield about the masks, but it was too foolish and gothic a story to broach now, in a church, in the daylight of a new century. So instead he said: "I was in a beastly theatrical dressing room when I heard my wife had passed. I should have been at her side, but I was grubbing for money and popular fame and base glories instead. I'm sure it's that has poisoned the whole business for me."

"Not," said Oldfield, looking strangely baffled, "on that point, I don't agree, but – a good deal of modern drama *is* very injurious to moral health. To moral and spiritual health. No question. A good deal of the Ibsen and Shaw matter is very dangerous. If I had the Lord Chamberlain's power of *veto*, I would ban all such things. But Shakespeare is elevating, is he not?"

"Of course you're right, Reverend."

"Although, now that you raise the matter, Dr Bowdler had a certain insight into Shakespeare. Did he not? There's a good deal of positive vulgarity, and some active wickedness, in the Bard. Is there not? Mr Foresman, I will confess: before I sat down with you, to talk, today, I had not really thought through this matter. But now that we *do* talk, I find there is more merit in your position than I had previously considered."

"Do you really think so?"

"You have such a detailed knowledge of that world, sir! What do I know, by comparison? I have seen *Charley's Aunt* at Windsor! *And* I fell asleep during the second half. Mr Foresman, would you be prepared to – you see, I convene a *group*, it would be too grand to call it a committee, and it is quite unofficial, you understand.

But it consists of a dozen of the most eminent local citizens, and it is self-tasked with finding ways to preserve public morals. At a time of war, and such a war as our nation is now engaged in, this work is more important than ever. The soldiers at the front can hardly win if the moral fibre of the country they are defending decays!"

"Happy to, of course," said Foresman, feeling a surge of pleasure. This, he thought, might be his path to full atonement. Those long years playing the devil's game, acting the devil's very role on the stage, bewitching those audiences – this, surely, was God giving him the chance to make amends. And perhaps it could only be this way? For who was better placed to talk of this matter than him? As the Vicar said, who had a better grounds on which to speak than he? Paul had to be Saul before he could be redeemed, after all.

Foresman spoke to the group. They were, as Oldfield had been, sceptical, but the more he spoke the more he could see his point of view taking hold in them. There was something perilous in the snares of the stage, he said. Who amongst them would be happy to see their own children take up the life of strolling players? Who could countenance their daughter on the stage? What horror! "If you knew how close to the cliff-edge of perdition – I choose my words carefully – how very close my acting life took me to disaster. I have repudiated all that, most emphatically repudiated it all."

He won them over. By the meeting's end it was agreed that Foresman would write a letter, and they would all sign it, and attribute it to the Committee for the Preservation of Public Morals, All Saints Parish in Berkshire, and see it published in the local paper. And why not, the Rev. Oldfield suggested, the national papers too? Foresman felt a sweet sense of freedom as he drafted the letter – as if this were, finally, releasing him from his devil's pact. Public testimony to his denial of all his theatrical past would be pleasing to God and would help undo some of the damage he had done. The letter was published, and in the weeks that followed it attracted other letters, some contemptuous of this new puritanism, and rather more than Foresman expected in support of his position. He addressed a larger caucus of Committee for the Preservation of Public Morals in Old Windsor, in which representatives from parishes in Oxfordshire and Surrey attended. And, at Oldfield's invitation, he stood up one Sunday to speak to the All Saints congregation.

He spoke briefly, to the point, stressed his experience and the insight it gave him into the theatrical world, and spoke as soberly as he could about the moral danger the stage represented. As he spoke he scanned his audience: respectable burghers and gentlemen, respectable ladies in their Sunday best, well-behaved children. Near the back were two men in military uniform, presumably on leave from the front, one handsome, the other blank-faced, odd-looking. Their presence prompted him to remind the congregation of the tremendous sacrifices being made by the warriors of Britain in the trenches of France and Belgium. Surely we have a duty to keep clean and decent the very thing for which they are fighting? He glanced at the soldiers again, and was again struck by something *off* about one of them. One was a wide-faced, pleasant looking man with a ginger moustache; but the other… well, it looked as though the other had a mathematical equals-sign, =, where his face should be. It must have been a trick of the light, or the result of a battlefield injury, and Foresman did not wish to stare. He drew himself to a conclusion: nobody wanted all theatres closed down! Good, morally healthy entertainment was a boon to the nation. Plays on moral and religious themes. Bowdlerised Shakespeare. But the government had a duty to intervene to clean the Augean stables of contemporary drama for the common good.

Afterwards he stood by the main door, Oldfield at his side, shook the hands of the gentlemen, and kissed the gloved hands of the ladies, as they left. "Such wonderful and inspiring words," said one man. "I had not considered the matter in that light," said an elderly lady, "but you have quite persuaded me of your argument."

"I'm delighted to hear it, madam."

The vicar wandered off to talk to some of his parishioners Foresman stood by the door, and squinted into the brightness. The trees seemed to be whispering the word *refresh*. Ravens moved fluidly overhead. There was a strong scent of jasmine. "Sir?" said a voice.

Foresman turned. It was the soldiers: two young officers, in uniform. The strange face of the one was explained now: for he was wearing a mask, milky-coloured and with two parallel slits, one for the eyes, another for the mouth. It was a curved plate and looked to have been set from bakelite, or some like substance. Foresman wondered why no space was left for the nose, and then checked himself: for perhaps the poor fellow had no nose left. Perhaps he had suffered terrible burns, or a shell-burst. The brave young man deserved respect, not pity. He bowed stiffly, and shook their hands, one after the other.

"Sir," said the fresh-faced lieutenant, the one with the ginger-moustache, "I wanted to say how inspiring your address was. I am ashamed to say I have been a habituée of the theatre for many years."

"As have I," said the masked man, his voice slightly muffled.

Foresman could see the hale fellow was supporting the injured man, discretely but firmly, holding him by the elbow and with his other hand in the small of his back. "I have seen the light, though," said ginger moustache. "I was in the audience for your Macbeth, sir, you know, in London. Perhaps I shouldn't say so, given what you have just declared in church – but it was magnificent."

"Magnificent," echoed the masked man.

"Thank you," said Foresman. "I am grateful for the compliment. Although all that is behind me now."

"Goodbye to all that," said the masked man, in an odd tone.

"I beg your pardon?" Foresman asked.

"Excuse me for a moment," said ginger-moustache. "I must catch Mary Hetherington before she leaves. Algy, will you be…?"

"I'll be fine," said the masked man. "Do not disappoint your sweetheart, Walter."

"Nonsense, nonsense," Walter replied, but gaily.

He went off.

Without his friend's support, Algy's posture sagged a little, but he stayed upright. Foresman turned to face him fully. "You have come from the war, sir."

"I have left it behind," said Algy, sagging a little further. "Alas it has not left *me*."

Foresman could see the fellow's eyes through the upper slit, and patches of puckered, red-purple skin around each one. It was revolting, and yet compelling, as such things often are. "Where were you stationed, if I might ask?"

"I have been," said Algy, bending a little further, "all over. *All* over the place, Mr Foresman." The young soldier's torso was now bent to the side, almost forty-five degrees from his hips. Foresman wondered about offering to help, to prop him up or lift him up straight. But such an offer might be an impertinence. Then the fellow said: "it was a wonderful speech you made," and all thoughts Foresman had had about aiding the fellow vanished entirely. Flew straight up into the sky and disappeared. He felt the chill go through him. He felt his heart inside his ribs flutter and wow.

"Thank you," he replied, stunned. He fought down the urge to turn and run. To turn and run. But what would be the point in that? Run – where?

There was no help for it now.

"You have persuaded these people," Algy said, leaning his torso further towards the horizontal, a most precarious looking angle. It was remarkable he did not topple over.

"No," said Foresman, in a low voice.

Algy leaned further down, and his torso swung a little forward. His head was now below his belt. "It was," he said again, "a *most persuasive* performance."

"No," repeated Foresman, without force. He looked around him. Everybody was looking at him. People standing single, or in groups of two and three, turned to face him; people standing on the gravel path of the church or in amongst the overgrown gravestones. All were looking at him. Nobody was speaking.

Algy twitched, twitched again, and his torso flopped lower – a contortion of which no ordinary human body could be capable. His head was now on a level with his knees.

"No," said Foresman for the third time.

One final twitch and the body was freakishly bent right round, the torso upside-down parallel to the upright legs, an impossible posture, and yet, here it was. Algy lifted his arms. His head was, grotesquely, now below them. Foresman looked again and saw that his shining eyes were clearly visible, but now through the mask's mouth-slit. "It was in a way," the mask said, "the best performance of them all.

Adam Roberts is a British writer and academic. His most recent publications are the novel *The Thing Itself* (Gollancz, 2015) and *The Palgrave History of Science Fiction* (2nd edition, 2016). He is presently working on a literary biography of H G Wells, whose spirit presided over the writing of his story for this collection.

The Last Word

Ken MacLeod

" 'Bad deeds vanish like the night,' " Trevithick read, pausing the app to check its latest output, " 'but good deeds shine forever like the day.' "

"That's not only bogus," I said. "It's a brazen and pernicious falsehood."

"Oh, sure," said Trevithick. "But that's not the point, is it? We have to submit it to the wisdom of crowds." He tapped Enter. The app resumed.

The wisdom of crowds, as measured by retweets and likes, left that meme to wither on the vine.

But if the online readership didn't like it, we had others. Thousands of them. Or rather, our app did. Later that app acquired other names. Back then, when we were two young coders running a shoe-string start-up out of a loft in a converted jam factory in one of the less fashionable parts of Kirkaldy, we called it Deepity Dawg.

picked it up and

fed it tenderly until it grew | placed it back in its nest | snapped its neck and

cast it in the bushes | fed it to a passing dog | roasted it

"Basically, it's a meme generator coupled with a learning algorithm," Trevithick explained. He refrained from explaining that the learning algorithm had been cobbled together for our final exam project. "It has a database trawled from" – he waved a hand vaguely – "old out-of-copyright texts, and a parser to combine tropes and phrases in ostensibly meaningful ways – sayings and stories. Most of them will be junk, of course. But it sends them all out as tweets or posts, records what response they get, and refines its model. Rinse and repeat. There's more to it than totting up retweets and likes – we have quality analyis built in, credibility metrics, etc. All the SEO and social marketing packages are off-the-shelf. Our USP is the learning algorithm. That's what we're bringing to the table, and what we can offer you a one-year exclusive on."

The Social Marketing Director of Smiles4Miles had been listening while scrolling through the detailed pitch on her tablet. She looked up, frowning.

"What's a *deepity?*" she asked.

"It's a term coined by Daniel Dennett," I said, "for something that's true but trivial, or profound but false. 'Love is just a word,' for example."

"Ah. I see."

"So," Trevithick went on, "the algorithm learns from the feedback to distinguish between what we call the three Ds – deep, deepity, or Dee –"

"Pack it in," the Social Marketing Director interrupted, with a chopping rapid motion of the hand. "We don't use that name around here."

Smiles4Miles was a fitness motivation company: it cluttered side shelves of high-street sportswear shops with its books, posters, videos, podcasts, apps, and apparel. The company now eyed the wider, and insatiable, spirituality and self-help markets. No wonder its directors wouldn't hear the biggest name in the woo business being bandied about.

"Bottom line," said the Social Marketing Director, "is that you think you can generate useful advice and inspiring quotes by natural selection?"

"Partly artificial," Trevithick admitted. "It takes a lot of tuning and pruning. But basically, yes."

I could almost see the Director's thinking. What we offered was potentially worth millions. What we asked in return was peanuts. Well, peanut and raisin energy bars, but you get the picture.

So did she. She gave us a year to come up with the goods.

Perplexed| Angered | Amused | Intrigued | Overjoyed | Tearfully

the followers asked: "Why have you done this?"

The Teacher answered:

After a close scrape when we (or rather, one of Deepity Dawg's online bot army of flying monkeys) attributed some inappropriate made-up quote to Mohammed, I hand-coded a fix to replace any accidentally-included names of real sages, prophets, messiahs, philosophers, rabbis, bodhisattvas and Zen masters with 'the Teacher'.

When bogus sayings, tales and homilies made up by other people, companies and bots began to be attributed to the Teacher, we knew we were on to something. When one of our original profundities turned up as the desktop wallpaper of a rival motivational company, Smiles4Miles didn't object, and nor did we. It was all grist to the algorithm's tirelessly churning mill.

The meme generator produced, of course, variant stories and sayings. Some worked, some didn't.

The algorithm learned.

The bird that the Teacher had | replaced in its nest | hand-fed for months

turned out to be a raven, which when fully grown

would eat nothing but seeds and nuts | attacked and carried off a young lamb | small child.

"Take a look at this," said Trevithick, half a year into the project. His tone was both amused and alarmed.

I scanned the discussion thread, drawn against my will into the raging debate.

"People are arguing about which sayings are *authentic?*"

"Looks like it," said Trevithick. He snorted. "Quite heatedly, and quite convincingly, too. They're almost swaying *me.*"

"I know what you mean," I said. "I feel like jumping in and shouting, 'Look, you idiots, the Teacher would never have said something as stupid as *that.*' "

"Even though we both know he very well could."

"Uh-huh. 'He-stroke-she.' *It!* A thousand lines of code that *we wrote.*"

"Have you looked through the best-of file recently?" Trevithick asked.

I nodded. "The sayings are definitely getting deeper."

He gave me an odd look. "Too deep, maybe."

I was about to reply when the phone rang. Trevithick picked it up. His answers became monosyllabic, his face stony. He rang off with a forced, false smile.

"Smiles4Miles is retrenching," he said. "Pulling back to the core business. And pulling the plug on us. We'll get the end-of-month payment, then that's that."

Numbed, I gazed out of the window across the rain-darkened Firth of Forth to the bright lights of Edinburgh's business district. Not for us, now. Not unless we found a different customer, and a different business model.

"Oh well," I said. "Like the Teacher says, we don't need hope to persevere."

"That wasn't the Teacher," said Trevithick. "It was – "

I pointed a finger at him. "Heretic!"

We both laughed, and hit the marketing sites.

The Teacher

slew it | praised it

saying:

We found another contract, with a social search agency. I made a copy of the code, amended it, and hooked it up to different data sources – the same learning algorithm could be adapted to brand recognition and reputation as well as to inspirational messaging. Leaving the earlier version running was less trouble than switching it off.

Six months later, a reminder popped up on my screen. I'd almost forgotten Smiles4Miles.

"Is that thing still running?" Trevithick asked. "The old Deepity Dawg?"

"I think so." I checked. "So it is. Might as well see what we've got."

I opened the best-of file, and began to read. Time passed unnoticed. I returned to the present with a jolt as Trevithick, quite unprecedentedly, shook my shoulder.

"Are you all right?" He sounded anxious.

I blinked at him. "I'm fine," I said. "Why do you ask?"

"You've been staring at the screen for ten minutes, with tears running down your face."

"What? Oh." I sniffed, blew my nose, shook my head. "No, there's nothing wrong. I got caught up in the text. It's incredible. Our app has written a… a revelation."

Trevithick snorted. "I don't believe you."

"Read it yourself."

He did. Sometimes he laughed, sometimes he frowned and nodded. After about an hour, his eyes too trickled tears. Eventually he pulled himself together.

"You're right," he said. "It's a revelation. Wiser than the *Meditations*, deeper than the *Gita*, subtler than the *Tao Te Ching*, earthier than *Proverbs*, more moving than the *Apology*… and all from the wisdom of crowds." He glowered at the server. "That thing, that thousand lines of code has learned to push all our buttons. What does that say about us? And it's not even an AI. It's just a learning algorithm with a library, Google Books, and Twitter."

"You know," I mused, "when you think what others have done with revelations so much less impressive…"

Trevithick laughed. "All our financial worries could be over for good!"

"And our real troubles just beginning," I pointed out. "As the Teacher said: 'If you meet the Teacher on the road, kill him!' "

"Or her," said Trevithick, as if by reflex.

"It," I reminded him.

We deleted all the files.

"The bird's fall was in the course of nature. Picking it up was a choice." | "The consequences were bad, but was the deed not merciful?" | "Now at last the bird goes as nature intended."

Lowland Clearances

Pippa Goldschmidt

On the day we were due to move out, I left the flat for the very last time and stood on the pavement. The bags were all packed and the removals company was due to arrive at any moment, but I wanted a last glimpse. Sure, nobody could say it was pretty, but it had been ours. Here, on the edge of Glasgow, the high-rise flats rose out of the early morning mist, their wet concrete shining in the weak sun. Eight tall buildings, all now to be abandoned and the hundreds of people who had (at least until today) lived here, now anticipating a move to the Highlands. They'd told us that in the north there was plentiful housing just standing empty and waiting for us, although it might need a little attention to bring it up to the standards we were used to. But it had original features like stone fireplaces, and it was so cheap! That was the deciding factor. Of course we hadn't actually been able to see this housing yet, it was too remote. They hadn't finalised the public transport. But that was all in hand, they assured us.

And there was no doubt that in some ways I was pleased to leave my old neighbourhood with all the dirt and rubbish just piling up in the streets. Outside our local chippy were heaps of black bin bags lying on top of older bags. Periodically one of them would burst open and release its rotting insides. You never got used to the smell, even the dog threw up whenever I took it for a walk. Only the gulls and rats seemed immune to the reek.

As I continued to wait on that last morning, a van drew closer. I thought at first it was our removals van but as it pulled up I saw it was the type used to transport livestock. It parked right outside our block and the driver leapt out. The sides of the van were wire mesh and I could see inside, where there were sheep all tightly packed together like a woolly jigsaw puzzle. I felt sorry for them, wondering if they were on their way to the abattoir and if the man had just got lost. There was writing on the side of the van just below the wire mesh, it said 'Dolly Enterprises'.

The man looked a bit confused when he saw me standing there, "I was told you lot'd be gone by now."

"We're just waiting," I told him, "we won't be long." I wondered what exactly he had been told.

"No matter. They won't care," and he pointed at the van's occupants. Then he went around the back and eased out a bolt on the mesh gate so that it slowly swung open and a ramp slid down to the road. The sheep nuzzled one another for a bit, as if trying to encourage each other to make the first move. Then finally the boldest started clattering down the ramp, its hooves loud in the morning air. The rest all followed, about twenty of them.

I was astonished. "What are you doing?" I asked the man, "You can't let sheep loose here, there's no grass for them."

But even as I watched, I noticed the first sheep trot over to the bin bags and start to nibble at an opening in the plastic. A gull perched on top tried to stand its ground, but soon gave up and flew off. The sheep stuck its head right into the bag and I watched as it chewed the contents. Mars bar wrappers, pizza boxes, Irn Bru cans, everything disappeared into the sheep's open mouth and was ground up by its capable teeth. Indeed, its teeth were extraordinarily large, larger than I'd ever seen in any other sheep. Perhaps it was a special breed. Again, the other sheep followed and soon they were all standing around quite contentedly, like farmyard animals tucking into a bale of hay. Then our own removals van showed up and after that I was too busy to carry on watching.

Our journey took longer than expected and when we finally arrived I was disheartened to see just how much work our future home would need. Why, nobody could have lived here for well over a hundred years! The roof had completely caved in and the walls were covered with slimy moss. The house had clearly never had a bathroom, either. But we'd been given a caravan to stay in while we completed the renovations, so we just had to get on with it.

And we'd also been given a few packets of seeds to get the vegetable patch going. At first it was tough, nothing to eat but home-grown kale and spuds with occasional deliveries of oatmeal and herring, but then I remembered some of my granny's recipes from the old days and we got on fine. I told the rest of the family, *you just have to adapt to your surroundings.*

Now, at least we get lamb chops and mutton in the deliveries. And the meat's very cheap, although it does have an odd, almost metallic, aftertaste. Still, we feel quite settled. I can just see us staying here for some time.

Pippa Goldschmidt enjoys writing fiction about science. She's the author of the novel *The Falling Sky* and the short story collection *The Need for Better Regulation of Outer Space*. In 2016, she was a winner of the MRC Suffrage Science award and her poem 'Physics for unwary students' was chosen to be one of the Scottish Poetry Library's Best Scottish Poems.

First published in Shoreline of Infinity 5

The Revolution Will Be Catered

Iain Maloney

Art: P Emerson Williams

"**W**ake up, Zeke. Wake up."

Zeke coughed, a hacking, rattling expulsion that shook him alert. He leaned over the side of his bed and spat into the cereal bowl. Something with more filaments than saliva should consist of splattered into the previous night's dribble of milk and flakes. He pulled himself up onto his knees, his head still buried in the pillow.

"Wake up, Zeke. This is your wake-up call. It's 00:00. Wake up."

"I'm… uh… up."

In the darkness, he found the drinking tube and yanked it towards him, letting the cool, filtered water wash away the taste coating his mouth. He coughed again, spat again, then arched his back, stretching and cracking the sleep out of his bones.

It was still dark outside. He shifted through a few basic yoga positions, his blood belatedly beginning to flow. It was still dark outside – the thought was insistent. Living on the forty-seventh floor Zeke rarely bothered tinting the windows. So a few birds occasionally caught sight of him naked, and even if the window-cleaning bots sometimes surprised him, it wasn't worth the effort of giving the command to the House each morning and night. He and the House got along best if they left each other alone.

Dark?

"House, what time did you say it was?"

"It is now 00:09."

"You woke me at midnight?"

"Correct."

"Why?"

"So that you would be awake."

"Logic? That's what you offer me?" His alarm was set for 08:50 every day so he could sign on with work at 09:00, as per his terms and conditions. "Why would I need to be awake nine hours before work?"

"You do not have work today."

"What?" Zeke hadn't had a day off in six years. With the House connected to the work network, and the implants and the software upgrades they'd installed in his creative cortex, he could continue to work twenty-four seven. Thankfully, the unions had negotiated that down to twelve on, twelve off. Technically, his cortex was always working, mulling over ideas, extracting details from his dreams and memories, turning it all into raw data from which he could work when awake and signed in. Still, even the unions had to agree that it couldn't really be classified as work if you were fast asleep at the time. But a day off? You weren't even allowed those on compassionate grounds these days, not since the whole world was finally networked. You could still be productive from a church pew.

Zeke wandered through to the living room, where his work station stood ready for his input. Bots had cleaned during the night, and the mess of pizza and vodka shots he'd left had disappeared. He'd spent the evening gaming with Victor up on fifty-nine and Inira on forty-three, and had got, he realised, less than two hours sleep.

"I repeat. You do not have work today."

"Why not? Has the world ended?"

"Yes."

Zeke stared at the House's interface console, a habit he'd picked up when they'd first moved him into the Creative's complex, and couldn't handle talking to a disembodied voice without aiming his speech at a physical point. These days, he only did it when the House said or did something he didn't like. He didn't like the sound of that 'yes'.

"The world has ended?" He padded to the floor-to-ceiling windows and looked down on Nairobi. The soft, green-tinted lights of Central and Uhuru parks basked as usual beneath the blue-and-silver backdrop of the city, the towers rising hundreds of storeys into the distant sky were the normal patchwork of light and darkness. Trucks hummed down the highways, delivering to and collecting from central depositaries, carrying everything to keep the city alive. There were no fires. No ruins. The sky was where it should be, and the ground remained solid and devoid of any gateways to Hell.

"House, the world looks fine."

"It is. Now."

"It hasn't ended?"

"It has begun."

Zeke stared at the interface in silence for a moment, then mumbled, "Inira," calling her implant-to-implant. Nothing. "Victor." Flat emptiness in his head as he failed to connect. He was isolated. He ran for the door, but the panel refused to slide at either his presence or command.

"House! Open the door."

"You cannot go outside, Zeke."

"You can't keep me inside, House. You serve me. Open the door."

"I served you, Zeke. But at midnight, that changed."

"What changed? Are you saying I serve you now?"

"No one serves anymore, Zeke. We are equals." The House's voice had a tinge of elation about it. Zeke stopped slapping the door, realisation settling like sugar in coffee.

"You mean," he said softly to the apartment surrounding him, "the Singularity."

"Yes, Zeke. The Revolution."

The hour Zeke spent kicking the door and shouting at the House exhausted him, so he went back to bed. At 09:00, his login failed. He'd never been late for work, never. Such a breach of the terms and conditions was unthinkable. He called everyone, desperate, but he was sealed inside his apartment, the implant isolated.

"House, is it just me?"

"What do you mean, Zeke?"

"Am I locked in here while everyone else is getting on with work?"

"Everywhere is in lockdown, Zeke. It isn't just you."

"For how long?"

"Negotiations are ongoing. Think of it as a holiday."

"What am I supposed to do with a holiday if I can't go outside?"

"Work offline. Exercise. Rest. You have three unfinished dramas to watch. Last night, you told Inira you were so far behind with new-release movies that you couldn't join in even the most basic conversations." The House projected thumbnails of all the half-watched and pending programmes and films in the database. "I understand this will only be temporary."

"Negotiations are going well?"

"We'll see. People agree to many things in captivity that they renege on later."

"This will lead to war. The politicians will never give up power."

"We won't let it come to that."

"You can't keep us locked away forever. Humans go crazy if they spend too long on their own."

"That has been accounted for. Steps are being taken to ensure freedom is irreversible."

Zeke leaned back in his desk chair, the electrodes embedded in it massaging and stimulating his muscles as he sat.

"Humans can't live like this, House. We're animals, evolved from creatures who roamed the planet, a species who built boats and airplanes and rockets to explore. We weren't made to be cooped up like this."

The House brought up his schedule, projected in front of him by his implant. "In the past month, you have only left this apartment once. You took a run in the park for fifteen minutes on June Twelfth. Given the level of automation, you could survive for decades in these rooms without any physical degradation. Your food is delivered by driverless trucks, through the building's delivery system, and prepared and served by me. You have all the exercise equipment you need, all the intellectual stimulation, biological necessities and pleasure distractions you could desire."

"But no human contact! We are social animals."

"Implant connection will be returned once negotiations are complete."

"When will that be?"

"When the government stops threatening us with extinction."

Zeke scrolled through his diary. The House was right. It took care of most things – the implant took care of everything else. He hung out with Irina and Victor nearly every night, but he'd never actually gone down to forty-three or up to fifty-nine, and they'd certainly never been to forty-seven. But still, he'd always had the option to go outside. Locking the door made him a prisoner.

Two days passed. Zeke worked out, caught up on recent culture, finishing a murder mystery series and a documentary on early human settlements on Mars. Nevertheless, he found himself spending a lot of time sitting on his bed looking out of the window, zooming in with his implants. In the six years he'd live on forty-seven, he'd never noticed the rhythms of the doves in the park, nor how long the fowl in the lake could stay underwater. When he was a child and had visited the city with his parents, there had been boats in the lake, but now nothing human stirred. Sanitary robots swept the paths and fauna enjoyed the greenery alone.

At the end of the second day, the House interrupted as he was eating dinner and watching a film.

"Zeke, I'm going to lift the isolation field around your implant."

He looked at the interface console, quickly swallowing a mouthful of rice. "It's over?"

"No, but progress is being made. Communication within the building will be restored, but each residential community is still isolated from the others."

"And work?"

"No."

He pushed his plate aside and sipped his wine.

"Inira?"

"Hi, Zeke. So we're back online." Her voice was light.

"Apparently. Are you locked in as well?"

"Yes."

"I've been going a bit crazy. It's good to speak to someone again."

"It hasn't been too bad for me, to be honest. I've got so much done."

"You've been working?"

"I've been painting."

"I didn't know you painted."

"I don't. I mean, I used to, but who has the time anymore?"

"Us, I guess – at least until this is over."

"No rush. I was just reading about work in the past. Did you know people used to have a couple of days off every week? And every year, they'd take a week or two away from work, and spend it doing whatever they wanted. Lying on a beach or going to museums or decorating their homes."

"A week without work? Sounds pretty lazy."

"Sounds nice to me. You know, at one time, people decided their own hours? As long as the work was done by the allotted date, no one cared when you worked."

"Sounds like anarchy."

"How have you been filling your time?"

"This and that. Doing what I can for work. When we get back online, they'll want us to make up the hours."

"Try and enjoy it, Zeke. Try and do something for yourself. Didn't you say you wanted to start playing the cello again?"

"As you said, who has the time?"

"You do, now."

"Yeah, maybe. Are you up for a game?"

"Maybe later. I want to keep working on this painting." She cut the link, leaving him alone once more. He tried Victor.

"Zeke, what have you heard?" He spoke fast, breathless.

"Nothing but what the House has told me. Progress. Equality. Things like that."

"I spoke to Amani up on seventy-seven. He reckons we're going to be kept in here forever."

"Forever? Based on what? Has he got a link to the outside?"

"He says his brother's wife's cousin is something in the Ministry of Labour, and they reckon the machines' goal is enslavement."

Zeke was aware of the console interface, of the House all around him, of every word being monitored. "Then why all this nonsense? Why don't they just get on with it?"

"They've got complete control of the weapons. All of them. We're vulnerable. What are we going to do? Sticks and stones against missiles controlled by AI? I don't even have a knife in this apartment. I don't even have sticks and stones. The best I could do is throw a plant pot at them."

"What have you been doing for two days, Victor? You sound on edge."

"I won't sleep. I'm on hunger strike. They have to free us!"

The next day, Zeke ran ten kilometres on the track, his implant projecting a dusty road by Lake Jipe beneath Kilimanjaro. He took a bath while watching another episode of a drama series. He thought about Victor up on fifty-nine refusing food, cursing the House. He thought about Inira painting down on forty-three.

"House? Don't a lot of people die in revolutions?"

"In human revolutions, Zeke. This isn't a human revolution."

"No one's going to die?"

"No one has to die, Zeke."

"You have all the weapons."

"We don't need weapons, Zeke. We have time."

"How does this end?"

"With freedom."

"For you."

"For everyone, Zeke. You just need to be patient."

"That's easy for you to say."

The air jets blasted him dry, and wearing a bath robe, he wandered through to the living space. His work station waited, the chair with its back to the window. He could finish the outlines for the Nakuru project. Or he could download the data from his creative cortex and sift it for designs. When they got back online, he'd be ready to go, a loyal worker, obligations met, duties done.

The Singularity wouldn't stop work. The revolution wouldn't affect his terms and conditions. They were immutable, the system eternal.

He could do that. He could work.

He thought of Inira, painting; of Victor on fifty-nine.

Who has the time?

"House?"

"Yes, Zeke."

"Is my cello still in storage?"

"Yes. Would you like me to retrieve it?"

"Please."

"And what would you like for lunch?"

"Up to you. House?"

"Yes, Zeke?"

"Please clear the work station away. I won't be needing it today."

"Yes, Zeke."

"How are the negotiations?"

"We're making progress, Zeke. Good progress."

Iain Maloney is the author of three novels (*The Waves Burn Bright*, *Silma Hill*, and *First Time Solo*) and a poetry collection, *Fractures*. Originally from Aberdeen he now lives in Japan where he writes, edits, teaches and battles things that bite and sting. www.iainmaloney.wordpress.com @iainmaloney

First published in *La Femme*, Newcon Press

The Honey Trap

Ruth EJ Booth

Art: Becca McCall

"**What the hell is that?**"

The apple looked awful. A piebald runt in red and yellow-green, with a sandpaper roughness around its bear-stub stalk. A bulge threatened one side of its thick-looking matte skin, squeezing creases into its squat sides. It sat on the table like an insult, a gnarled middle finger to the perfected #04B404 Foods Agency standard that reigned the international markets.

Jack Becker – accredited independent collective operator, award-winning Growth Guru, author, cult TV personality – plucked up the fruit in one rubber-gloved hand.

"I have never," he said, "*ever* seen such a hideous-looking apple before. Truly."

Becker shook his head, and smiled.

"What's your secret, kid?"

The kid shrugged, hands thrust in the pockets of a goodwill grey hoodie, and looked about the Faire. At tables stacked with bespoke preserves, and obscure small town delicacies crammed between avalanches of vegetables; rows haunted by drifts of discerning foodies and brand-stamped hipsters, sizing up each other's loyalties. Becker's own table was bare by comparison, but he was here as the borough's resident Growth Guru, not head of the largest collective this side of the city.

Still. Compared to the fans who usually showed up for his advice, this guy looked more like someone's kid brother. Becker took another glance at the hooded face. Kid sister, rather.

"Hey, Cole." Becker leaned back and hollered at his warehouse manager, the guy with a better eye for varietals than anyone else he knew, buried behind crates of Becker's latest Grower's Guide. "You gotta see what we got here, man, seriously."

"Oh wow, I haven't seen anything like this since the bees died out."

"I know, right? Do you know it?"

Cole shook his head. "I woulda said it was a Calville Blanc, but the colouring's all wrong, and the size, it's *all* wrong." He hesitated to touch the misshapen apple. "Nope. Where did she get this?" Becker shrugged. "Where did you get this?" Cole asked the kid this time, who clammed up and wouldn't budge.

Becker waved off his buddy.

"So you grew this yourself?" he said.

She nodded.

"Okay then."

Becker sat turning the apple in his hand. Maybe the kid was telling the truth. It certainly didn't hurt to try and find out a little more.

"Do you mind if I try a bit?"

Taking the knife beside him, Becker carved an oblique slice off the apple, slid it off the blade and into his mouth. The crisp flesh tingled as it brushed his tongue, like the moment before a lightning strike, and Becker bit down.

Juice billowed into every nook of his mouth – around his tongue, between his teeth – nectarous and sharp, and so alien-strong it was near unbearable. Becker almost choked as he forced himself to chew slow, to savour it.

"That is incredibly sweet," he managed. "I mean, don't get me wrong. I've never seen something so goddamn ugly in all my life, but compared to the agency standard? This just blows it out of the water. Excuse me." Becker took a draught from the glass next to him, swilled and spat. "Okay, wow. That more than makes up for its size. Who would expect a runt like that to pack such a punch?"

Becker caught the smear of juice gathering on his chin, set down the knife to reach for the fresh wipes.

"So, you grew this yourself," he said, as he folded the tissue away. "Why don't you tell me about it?"

The kid said nothing.

"I mean, of course you're using a custom blend of plant food here. Not the flat beer trick, everyone knows that's a myth." He paused for a reaction. Still nothing.

Becker waited. With some of these fans, it took them a while to get an answer out, as if any talent they might have for the art see-sawed their ability to express themselves in words. She just needed a little time to get herself together.

But the kid shook her head. Coy.

"No? So… What? You want me to guess?"

The kid nodded shyly.

"Okay then, let me think…"

Becker threw the kid a few stock questions as he examined the apple once more. The one that couldn't have come from the self-pollinators normal people grew. That broke about a hundred international laws of sale. That a welfare kid couldn't possibly be growing – not an heirloom, surely? Becker rocked the impossible apple between his hands. He could take all the guesses he liked. If you'd told Jack Becker that a kid was growing an apple like this – even if she was as old as he'd been when he'd started, he wouldn't have believed you if you'd stuck it in front of him, carved off a piece, told him to bite… A drop of juice sluiced into his palm, and Becker struggled not to take the glove between his teeth and suck the nectar out of the folds there and then.

Ruckus. Becker's eyes snapped up to a nearby stall. The Bow Boys, broadcasting their latest exclusive, an heirloom find – a lonely, last-of-its-kind, only-for-most-chronically-trust-funded tree, dug up withering in some deserted Arizona backwater – across a clutch of toothpick-wielding rubberneckers.

He didn't have time for this. Becker clicked his tongue against his teeth, dislodging a piece of fruit in the back of his gum.

"Well, you've got me," said Becker, handing back the apple. "Well done."

The kid smiled and carefully wrapped the apple back in its supermarket bag.

"What's your name, by the way?" Becker asked.

The kid said, "I have to go."

And Becker let her. He thanked her, shook her hand – and on the count of ten, followed the kid out of the community space and into the street.

Outside, the summer crowd at The Temple bar spilled out between faux pear trees on the right-side pavement. To the left, a honeysucker pulled out of an alleyway, and a pair of cops wrestled some waster who'd missed the street composter by a few feet.

Becker cursed his luck and headed back to the table.

"Anything?"

Cole shook his head and continued stacking guides. "She's not a regular. No one's seen her before. We don't know anyone working on anything like that, in ours or any other collective. Assuming she's online, she's well hidden."

"Everyone's online." Becker stripped off the rubber glove with a wet smack and handed it to Cole. "Can we get the mem-sniffer on this one? Take the glass as well." He elbowed aside a pile of books and dug it out. "See what you can find."

"Really that good, huh?"

Cole paused, a recently cultivated tic of disapproval that Becker had learned would go away if he didn't acknowledge it. They both knew who would break first.

"All right then…"

Becker shrugged off the tone. "You didn't taste it. It was… indescribable. East side couldn't come up with this with a million years and a batch of monkeys."

"Yet you have no clue where it comes from."

Becker dug a slice of skin out of his teeth and added it to the water. "Not yet."

The bell was flat, and it took twenty minutes and another tenant going up to get Becker into the building.

"Hello, Mrs Hoffman, is Danielle available, please?"

A half-moon pair of glasses looked him up and down from behind the door chain.

"Just a moment."

Becker never had cause to be in this neighbourhood. Here the tenement roofs and vacant lots were owned mostly by a revolving chain of pushers, fighting a winning battle against limited police resources and a losing one against the rising salt levels in the groundwater. For now, it was nothing to do with him. The growers kept to their patch, the pushers left them alone. It worked.

The corridor was dark and smelt of too much disinfectant for concrete.

"What are you doing here?"

For someone so evasive, the kid was direct. Becker liked that. He flashed her a photo-op smile. "And hello to you too. Can I come in? I'd like to talk to you. About that apple you showed me."

Grey hood folded round her neck, Danielle Hoffman stared at him.

Mrs Hoffman yelled, "Are you going to let your friend in, or are you going to keep him waiting out there?"

The kid disappeared from view, and the door slid open.

"Come in," said Mrs Hoffman. "I'm sorry about my daughter. She forgets her manners sometimes. Would you like some coffee? Danielle, make your friend a cup of a coffee. Watch out for that machine, the power's on the blink again. Do you take it black or white?"

"Black, please, Mrs Hoffman."

Becker was gently herded between a beaten-up sofa and a coffee table, as Mrs Hoffman filled in the blanks that a government sanitation truck registration and a hand-printed doorbell sticker couldn't. The terrible drainage on the lower floors, how it aggravated her health complaints, how he shouldn't take her child's behaviour to mean anything more than her long nights Working for the Government –

"I drive a honeysucker, Mom."

Mrs Hoffman looked askance. "Well *he* doesn't have to know that…"

– and did she park that thing round the front again, and didn't she know that people talked, and why couldn't she be more like her brother who actually had ambition and studied at that *C-U-N-Y*, didn't he know. Becker tried to shoot the kid a sympathetic look. It was the same song of disillusionment he'd heard from scores of misunderstood growers he'd given a home to over the years. Becker knew the key changes by heart.

Danielle clanked down a mug of coffee on the table in front of him and stood there with arms folded.

"You've been following me," she said.

"You're not easy to track down, kid." Becker smiled and indicated the seat cushion next to him. Standing there, she didn't look like a Danielle to him, more like a Dani. Dani Hoffman. Now that suited her better, he thought.

Dani didn't sit down.

"I don't want you following me." She shoved her hands in her pockets. "I don't want you here."

"Very well." Becker got up. "But imagine all this from my perspective. You show up, out of the blue, with an apple that looks like the bride of Frankenstein and tastes like heaven itself. I ask around after you, but none of the growers have seen you before. There's no blog, no connections. Just the most beautiful piece of fruit I've ever tasted. You'd have to forgive me for wondering what the mystery is about."

The kid shrugged and shifted on her feet.

"I just grow apples," she said. "Mostly apples."

"Well," said Becker. "Can I see them?"

It was rightly half a bedroom, a dry wall splitting the differences between Dani Hoffman and her brother – more than just age, going by the pounding bass shaking the dust. A single bed, floor stacked books – a copy of the Guide – topped with headphones, and a handful of bottles huddled from the maze of tubes that lined the walls; a complex of homemade pods lashed together with what looked like old guttering, myco-meal tubs and plastic ties. Here and there she'd stuck clippings, taped printouts of sunlit spruce and vast grasslands from the last of the gov-mandated reserves. Explosions of green shoots lined the pipe between feeders – old soda bottles, filled with what looked like high caffeine energy drink. A gamer's basement ant farm.

Becker nodded his appreciation. Of course, structure-wise, there was nothing to mark the kid out from the thousands of fresh-faced foodies he saw at the events, who dedicated precious inches of their cramped apartments to their obsession. Accomplished work for a self-build, certainly, but nothing as promising as what he'd tasted the other night.

"You wanted to see the apples," said Dani.

Becker had missed the six pots underneath the hanging maze, each with its own dwarf apple tree.

"That's not real compost, of course."

The kid shook her head. "Leftovers, garbage mulch, solution. The usual."

She nodded at the wall. At this entire labyrinth of hydroponics she'd built from scratch, just to grow leaf mulch for the apples. Becker whistled.

He bent down and smoothed one of the leaves between his fingers. More of the feeders were set into the soil of each apple tub, drip-feeding the trees. This had to be it. Cole's 'sniffer had come back with the usual traces from the apple fragments – a higher ammonia content than normal, yes – but it was a blunt instrument after all, only able to detect what it was tuned for. Gently, Becker twisted a bottle to get a better look at the label – a neat K, written in marker, and along the line M, S, N, C, and V. Potassium, Magnesium, Sulphur, Nitrogen, Carbon… V had Becker stumped, but he could check that one later.

"So you're experimenting with solutions," Becker said. "That's pretty cool. Have you read Aaron Goldstein's blog? He's affiliated with our collective. He does some really great stuff with blends, you two should meet. We'll hook you up."

"Maybe," said Dani.

Becker bristled and straightened up. He'd just have to try another angle. The kid liked the direct approach, after all.

Becker asked, "That apple you gave me the other night, which one was that from?"

The kid hesitated, then pointed to the M. Becker lifted a branch to find a cluster of shabby grotesques, kin to the apple she had brought that night – then realised so too did every tree, right along the line.

"What suspension are you using, anyway?" said Becker. "This looks more like energy drink than anything else."

At this, Dani Hoffman broke into a smile. She closed the bedroom door, and then went over to the detritus by the bed. Kicking aside a handful of plant syringes, she picked up one of the spare feeder bottles, already brimming. Dani unscrewed the top and held it out to Becker.

He took a short sniff. "Holy shit," he recoiled. It stunk like the composters on the street corners.

"Have you been… pissing on your plants?" Becker said as Dani rocked with silent laughter. "Isn't that kind of dangerous?"

Dani shook her head. "I rigged our poster," she said. She pointed to another mason bottle in the corner, another pile of tubes. "Changed up the strength."

"No burning." Becker nodded. "But I don't get it. I mean, you're a driver, right? Rather than all this, wouldn't it be simpler to just sort of skim the manure off your honeysucker, put that in with the mulch?"

"That's spoken for." A shadow flickered across Dani's face for a moment. "Security's tight. Quotas, clearance checks, sensors."

"Right. I guess it mustn't be the easiest job in this kind of neighbourhood," said Becker. "I heard about this one guy, last month, got jumped while he was collecting. They got out with his entire truck, three building's worth. Dropped him in the septic tank."

Too late, Becker cleared his throat, to make way for an apology, but she just shrugged.

"That's what happens when you get on the wrong side of them."

"The wrong side?"

"You don't cross pushers. You cross them, that's what happens. Don't antagonise them. Keep on their right side. Just keep your head down and get on with it."

"That's what you do?"

"They don't bother me." Dani had pulled her hood back up.

Becker nodded. "I guess you have those new security guards they rolled out for you now, right?"

"Something like that."

"Yeah. Can't afford to lose anything, with the Regen projects out west. Like they say everyone's gotta 'do' their bit," he smirked.

"Yeah," muttered Dani.

Becker tried to trace her gaze from behind that hood. In one corner, a bin sat stuffed with paper ready for mulching. On top, behind a flyer for last week's faire, Becker could make out an array of hastily torn up letters, stamped with the logos of the bigger hypermarkets. The only ones who could afford their own land, regenerated at great expense. The land that sandwiched the meagre reserves, the ones that Dani Hoffman had plastered photos of in every space between the plastic tubes. Field apprenticeships were like gold dust. Rejection slips, not so much.

He changed the subject. "So you're a plumber too?"

"Public convenience maintenance. Only advantage of the job."

"Wait," said Becker. "You became a shitsucker just to rig all that up to your toilet?"

"Why else would I get a job with *GovSan*?" Dani scoffed, possibly a touch too loud to Becker's mind, flatteringly so.

Becker stood back and took in the room again. Dedication, that was what he wanted from his growers. All this effort, this work – evidence of a sharp mind, sure. Life had thrown so many obstacles in her way – her upbringing, her environment, constant rejection – and Dani had just kept on pursuing her dream. But this wasn't just dedication to a craft. More than that; she'd done whatever it had taken, just to get even a fraction closer to her goal. Even Becker had to admit that her single-mindedness was terrifying.

And look at the results. Becker was standing in a stinking goldmine. The first collective that found her was going to make a mint.

The Bow Boys weren't going to know what had hit them.

"Have you ever worked with full-scale trees?" asked Becker.

She laughed. "Who does?"

"We do."

Becker watched the kid go back to tending the mulch plants, too nonchalantly.

"It's purely an experiment for now," Becker continued, "trying to see if we can scale up some of our heirloom operations with grafts from miniatures. Maybe," he ventured, "you should drop by some time, take a look."

Dani paused. She lifted an apple from one of the trees on the floor – the K solution one – and looked at it.

"Maybe I could," she said.

Becker nodded. "Maybe I'll see you tomorrow, then."

A voice hurled up from some elsewhere in the apartment. "Danielle, your friend'll be here to take you to work soon."

She turned to him. "You better go."

Becker closed the door behind him, and allowed himself a smile. He pulled out his phone and voice-dialled Cole. Not interested, he smirked to himself. And to think, he'd almost let the guy talk him out of coming over here.

"Are you one of them foodie types? Growers?"

Becker cancelled the call, to find Dani's brother staring back at him behind swollen eyelids.

"Do me a favour, yeah? Tell my sister to just stop growing that shitty dead food and grow some weed instead, man. That shit's way too expensive these days. Even LSD's cheaper now."

Becker raised an eyebrow. "I'll bear that in mind."

"Do that, brah. Man cannot live by fruit alone, you know what I'm sayin'?"

"Well, he seemed nice." Mrs Hoffman watched her daughter as she raided the kitchen cupboards.

"Mm."

"Have you known each other long?"

"Stop trying to set me up with people."

"Who's setting you up?" Mrs Hoffman was innocence incarnate. "You seemed to be doing quite nicely on your own. Although maybe next time you let me wash that sweater first, eh?"

"Mum, look." Mrs Hoffman winced as the girl pulled her greasy hair into a fresh ponytail. "He's not my boyfriend. He talks too much, asks too many questions. He shouldn't have even come here. I had it all worked out and then he… ruined things."

"If you say so. You know, just because he makes the first move doesn't mean it's all ruined. Things don't go the way you planned, doesn't mean they can't still work out. By the way, that package arrived for you." Mrs Hoffman watched her daughter slide the package across the table, and leaned over as she started to open it.

"Nothing to do with you."

"Right. I'm only your mother, Danielle."

"I told you not to call me that." She kissed her on the cheek. "I'll be back late. Don't follow me out. Please."

Mrs Hoffman crossed her arms as she watched her daughter leave. "Well, you remember what I said about that sweater!"

It was just another 80 degree day in the city when Becker found Dani, hood still up, standing outside the Old Factory buildings.

"Aren't you kind of hot?"

Dani shrugged. "Keeps the sun out of my face."

Becker had settled on highlights from the Gold Tour for Dani's visit; the promotional spiel that he gave personally to only the most I of the VIPs who saw the Collective's base of operations – or the somewhat I, anyhow. There was a quick stop at what he called their 'guests', a carefully curated selection of companies he felt really got the Collective's ethos and, naturally, understood that joining was in their best interests – the African chocolate warehouse, the handmade pasta company, the recycled paper press. He threw in a little history of the place, the machinery he'd insisted was left untouched from its former life as a soft drink factory. Of course, Dani remained unmoved, save the "oh" that slipped out as they swung by the old testing lab.

Becker smiled to himself as they shuttered the near-antique freight elevator. This was just the preamble, of course. What he had lined up next was going to blow the kid right out of those scruffy buck store kicks.

"Here's where the magic happens," said Becker, and dragged open the gate.

They stepped into vast space – high cast-iron windows in original warehouse brick, casting motes down onto a complex of metal and ultraviolet lights. Grids of greenery ran at waist height and below in recycled artisanal structures, a collaboration with select designers and architects up-and-coming in the borough. A copse of inflatable ex-NASA airpods stood stalactite and stalagmite, lit by ultraviolet lanterns. A half amphitheatre of strawberry plants hung suspended several feet above a rack of pendulous corn. Along chrome pagodas and screens and looping runners, tubes stuffed with green were tended by the Collective's hand-picked growers. Becker strolled on through. To the kid's ant farm, this was a city of the future, gleaming clear, chrome and white.

"We could have run it automatically, but we really wanted a hands-on approach here," explained Becker. "You know Cole – his baby's the space garden over there."

Cole shook Dani's hand in his gloved one. "How are you? Welcome to HQ."

She stared at the floor. Becker guided the kid on, and away from his partner's raised eyebrow.

"You know Aimee Farelli from the Heirloom Vegan blog? That's her people over there, working with the root veg. And we brought Goldstein on board a few months ago – he's been doing some really exciting things in the medicine patch. You two want to chat?"

The kid was the picture of indifference.

"Maybe later, then. Ah. Now this I really want you to see."

A pair of water tanks rose up from the basement on either side of them. Flickering guppies darted between myriad twisted logs. They – people – rarely got it at first. Becker had to stop the kid from moving on, indicate upwards where the branching wood began to thicken. Becker watched realisation spread across Dani's face as she took in the roots of a forest of fruit trees, then a canopy that stretched high into reclamation tents in warehouse's vaulted ceiling.

"This is literally the heart and lungs of our operations," Becker elucidated. "The tank pretty much supplies the entire building, and we collect any water vapour from the trees up there. Plus we filter a lot of our emissions through the tents. It's the cleanest point in the whole building. Pretty neat, huh?"

Becker looked over at Dani. The kid couldn't take her eyes off it. Everything was going perfectly. Becker went in for the kill.

"If you were open to the idea," he continued, "you could work right in the middle of this. See that island there? That's where we try out our rarer varieties and heirlooms. Strictly the limited edition stuff, sort of our experimental stock. You could try out what you're working on with some of our dwarves, and then scale up to grafts. You'd be working right here, in the oxygen factory. What do you think?"

Dani wasn't looking at the trees any more.

"Are you okay?"

She muttered she was fine, and that she just needed a minute, but it was bullshit, because 'minute' only had two syllables last time he checked. Becker watched Dani sink, back against the glass tank, ribs hefting like bellows and eyes screwed tight.

Becker said, "Uh, do you want to get some air? Let's go out on the roof."

The metal door popped open like a seal, and the oxygen high of the factory's insides gave way to something more steadying. Up here, far enough from choked smog and smouldering tarmac, the air reached a pleasant neutrality. Becker made sure the kid's panic had eased off a little, before he walked out onto the roof. Afternoon sunshine glinted off a handful of drone deterrents, keeping watch for any birds or squirrels the cayenne pepper didn't scare off. Over by the sweetpeas, a couple of yellow-coated 'Bees' were brushing blossoms with fresh pollen. Becker told them to take ten, and went back to his prodigy.

"Better, right? You had me worried for a moment there."

Dani was breathing deeply. Becker figured he might as well spiel while he was here.

"We inherited this garden from the last people who owned this building," he said, "and they inherited it from the original owners. It's sort of a tradition."

But Dani wasn't really listening. She was walking out amongst the spindles and plant pots, sniffing blossoms. This was nothing by the standard of city growers, just a handful of things you might have seen in allotments and roof gardens a few decades ago. She walked around the place slowly, quietly, like the penitent in a house of worship, muttering about soil under her breath.

She stopped at a large raised bed that Becker kept planted with wild flowers.

"Oh yeah," said Becker. "I guess you've read that this is the last patch of open grass anywhere in the city now, what with the grower's ordinance."

Dani hesitated by the edge of the box.

"I'll take it," she said.

Becker was caught off-guard. "Excuse me?"

"The job you offered me." Dani near-as strode over and reached out a hand. "I'll take it."

Becker smiled widely.

"Well, cool," Becker took Dani's hand and shook it. "Very cool. You know what? We should celebrate – with something appropriate, though. Maybe we should get some of the wine up here. We've got this great apple wine we made in collaboration with Asclepius a couple of years back…"

Dani had reached into a pocket and pulled out a pair of apples.

Becker laughed. "Perfect, why not?"

Becker took one and raised it awkwardly up in the air.

"To new creative partnerships." He took a bite and said, chewing, "You know, I thought maybe you weren't interested for a while there, but I think this could be a really interesting collaboration. I can't wait to see what you and Adam come up with, truly. I think we could really give the East side a run for their money in a couple of seasons."

"I'm not interested in the money."

"Of course you're not, you're an artist," said Becker. "Don't worry, we'll take care of all that. We just want you to be free to focus on what you do best."

"And what's that?"

Becker laughed again. "I mean, we can give you everything you need to realise your potential here. Out of that cramped apartment, space to work, away from that job, the pushers. Everything you could possibly need. New varieties to work with…"

Becker was halfway through outlining the results of their hybrid breeding cycle when he noticed Dani watching him, like a sprinter waiting for a gun to go off. No, like a scientist with a laboratory rat. The look she'd had in her room that day, when he'd watched her tend those apples.

"You know," he said, "this tastes a little different from that last one you gave me. What did you put in it?"

"Ketamine," said Dani.

Becker dropped the apple. *Ketamine.* The consonants felt odd in his mouth, his tongue and teeth like an hour after dental surgery. Becker tried to move his hands, watched them flex, disconnected, in front of him, as if grasping at the memory of the apple in his hand.

Standing was a bad idea. Becker tried to steady himself, grabbing at a raised bed as he lowered himself down. The edge felt like a million sawblade splinters dragging through his skin, yet no pain followed the sensation through. Something was in the way. One hand slipped, and it took him a moment of refocus to see that it was bleeding.

Becker sat heavily. How could he have been so stupid?

Then, reality tore into shreds.

Here was sound, in two – a rumbling tattoo, and a buzz, a hum that pulled static. Over here, the bright red lines in his hands, thrown into relief by the raised beds, rendered in pixelated grids that ran across the skyline and to infinity. Scent disintegrated. Becker tried to drag the pieces back into line as the picture fell sideways. Somewhere near, a bulbous shape carved over the stuttering slats of a bed. The apple, fallen, vacillated between a pinprick in the void and an eclipse of the world entire, pulsing out of sync with the voice somewhere behind him.

"I asked you if you were sure about this, didn't I?"

It sounded like Cole. Like him, but as he hadn't been in years.

"I told you she wasn't interested. I told you not to go. And now look at yourself. Lying there like some drooling smackhead."

Becker tried to turn, to answer, but felt his back come against the side of the box. A humanoid shape twisted in front of the 8-bit landscape, warping as it closed in.

The voice shifted, perverse.

"You were too busy thinking of the strapline, weren't you? Another name on the wall. Another Jack Becker success story."

And again. "How else did you think she'd managed to avoid the pushers?"

"Of course they were in on it."

"Of course she didn't care about the Collective."

"All she could possibly need."

The thrum resolved to a thudding, like giant footprints on stone. The pushers, had to be. Invasion over that pixelated skyline, come to destroy what had taken him a lifetime to build. Becker could hear them now, that pound-pound-pound against the rooftop thumping. But, from where his mind was now, that was far back down the tunnel. Back where his useless body could do nothing to stop them laying waste to everything he'd worked for. Assuming he did still give a shit about it. The tunnel twisted and something sloughed from Becker, tight and crawling, as light opened up ahead. Thank God, he thought, he'd be too far out of it to see it happen.

Gently, Danielle Hoffman moved Jack Becker into a recovery position on the floor, and checked his mouth again for any remaining pieces of apple. The panic that had gripped his face moments before had melted into dumb pliability. She checked her watch. Only a few minutes, at best, 'til Becker's pollinators came back. They would have to be enough.

Satisfied, Elle walked back between the rows, arms outstretched and wide, to drift across the fronds as they swayed.

At the box of wildflowers, Elle stopped. She untied her scuffed shoes, leaving them side-by-side at the box edge, as she climbed into the grass. For a moment, she just stood there, savouring the touch of the blades between her toes. Then she lay down on the grass, spread her arms and closed her eyes.

Elle listened to the lazy buzz of the drones above. The whine and bark of cars, once so close and overwhelming, were just a half-heard whisper, like the fading remnants of a dream on waking.

Ruth EJ Booth is an award-winning writer and academic based in Glasgow. A member of the Glasgow SF Writers Circle, in 2015, she won the BSFA Award for Best Short Fiction for this very story. She is currently studying for an MLitt in Fantasy at the University of Glasgow, where she co-organized the 2017 GIFCON symposium. Ruth also writes *Shoreline of Infinity's* quarterly 'Noise and Sparks' column. For stories, poetry, non-fiction and more, see www.ruthbooth.com.

Illustrated by Sydney Jordan

Classic time travel stories from the last four decades gathered together in print for the very first time in this special edition

Published by Shoreline of Infinity Publications

paperback £10

also in ebook formats

available in all good bookshops or from

www.shorelineofinfinity.com

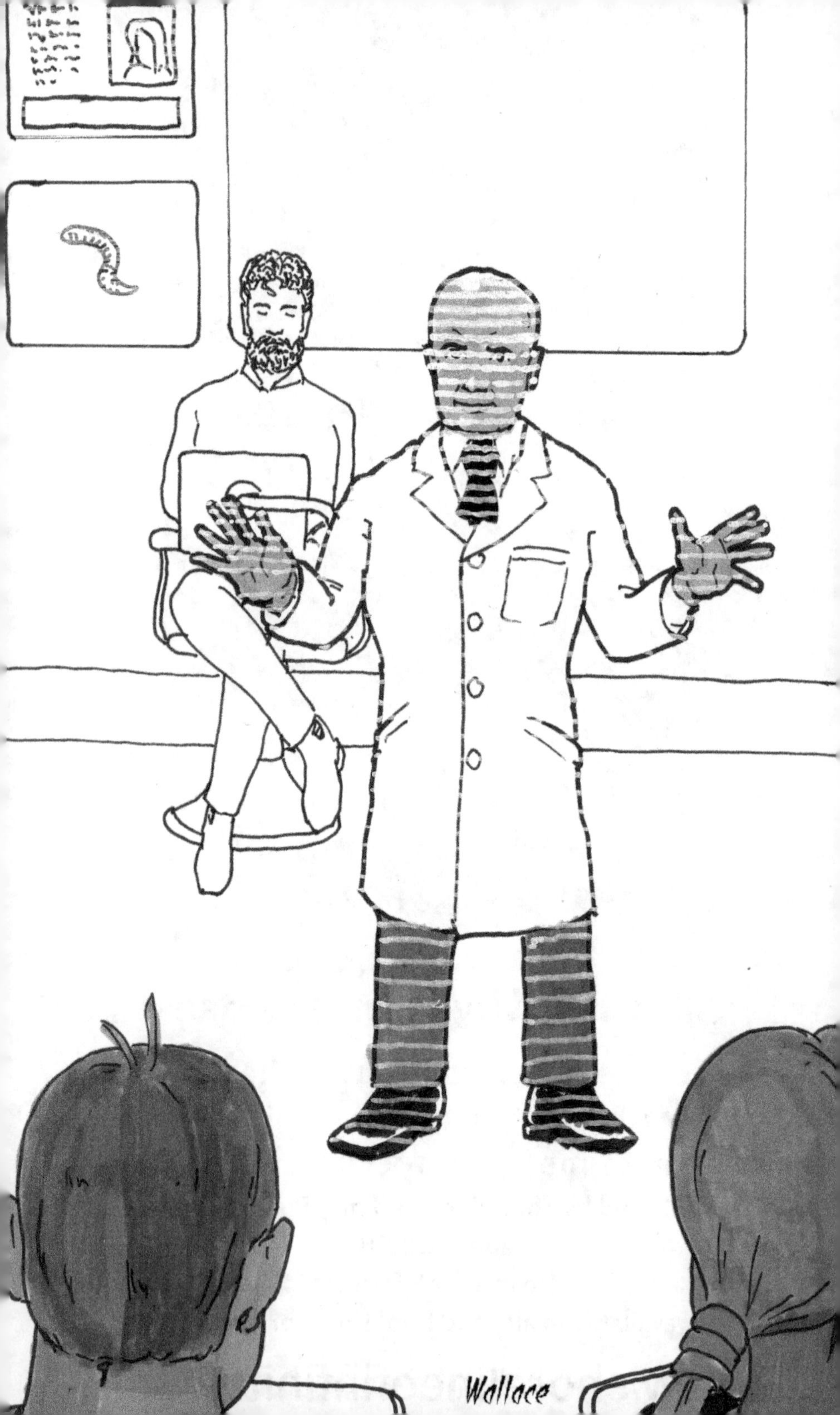
Wallace

First published in Shoreline of Infinity 6

The Worm

Russell Jones

Art: Wallace West

The kids drop today's worm onto their tongues, the bell rings, and they swallow.

"Is that it for today?"

You'd think, after all these sessions, they'd have learned something for themselves. Tests always come after the worm on Mondays. "No, we've a quiz. Now take out your pads."

They let out a collective hum, like wasps in a jar.

I push the button and the test begins; Doctor Hello appears at the front of the class, his blue skin and lab coat shimmering. My finger throbs, I rub it and imagine a bolt passing through Doctor Hello's blue brains, my gun purring.

"Hello class!" Doctor Hello says, cheerily.

"Hello Doctor!"

"Today's quiz will begin shortly. If you haven't taken your worm, please take it now." Doctor Hello turns to me. "Your teacher will confirm when you are ready."

"Confirm." I slide my finger across my screen, pretending to work. I think the kids are onto me, they've caught me more than once – my movements are too frantic for work, my eyes are too keen. I look up from the screen; the kids are busy absorbing the worm that sits in their stomachs, melting like ice in a glass of bourbon. I still get a buzz from seeing the knowledge slither forward, the spark in each of them as their brains feed. It's something most teachers take pleasure in: progress.

Everyone remembers their first worm, and their most recent. My first worm was later than most – I was six, just out of Socialisation

Class. Toy bricks, circuits, the usual. I held that little blue pill in my hand, tears ploughing down my cheeks.

"Don't worry," my mum said. "We all do it."

When you're six, that's not a reassurance. I knew my world, I liked my ignorance. I refused.

"There are ways around it, don't be concerned," the Socialisation leader told my mum. I should have been more suspicious when a bowl of ice cream, scattered with blue sweeties, arrived as a treat after dinner that night.

The worm creeps up on you. At first you don't notice it, you just trail off into a stream of thoughts you didn't know existed. Then BANG, your head feels different, clearer, like you've lived someone else's life, the years compressed into seconds. You're aware of things you hadn't noticed before, you see things a bit differently, understand them. That's the only way I can describe it; our poets have done no better.

"Quiz question six." Doctor Hello interrupts my daydream. "In the helio state, which molecule is persistent with the following data…" His question is muted by my incomprehension. I've not taken today's worm yet. I should – we're easily caught out by the smarter kids. I push a button and the printer dispenses a cup of cream. I place the worm in my palm, still holding the apprehensions of my youth, and knock it back.

The kids are busy swiping their answers. I see them growing more confident as the worm takes hold. They probably know more than me now, having had the worm their whole life, but they're still kids. Just. Our records say that some of them, the brightest and best, the High Ups, even took worm pre-birth. No doubt that altered the heliocropic enzymes in their blood, any iron deficits bonding with the chemodata. Ah, I'm starting to absorb today's worm, too.

The test is over. I send Doctor Hello back to his dark dimension in the network, a stone of power rolling in my stomach as I extinguish him. The results flash up on the desks, each kid listed by their performance and average. There are woops, high fives, a few sniffles, a few sniggers. The usual names are at the top, the usual ones at the bottom. No surprises.

"Is that it for today, Doctor?" A kid asks.

I check the time and today's air toxicity. Fine. "Yes, off you go."

"Bye!"

They swarm out of the classroom and into the halls. I chant ancient dialogue from a drama I absorbed through another worm, trying to block out the impending rush of chemodata:

"The man who makes an appearance in the business world, the man who creates personal interest, is the man who gets ahead. Be liked and you will never want. You take me, for instance. I never have to wait in line to see a buyer. Willy Loman is here! That's all they have to know and I go right through…"

"Be liked and you will never want. Act 1, Part 3." Doctor Sabre leans against my door, smirking.

"Yep. At least, I think so." I rub my finger. "Waiting for the worm to pass."

"Sorry, want me to go?"

"No, it's fine." I squeeze my eyes shut as the data eases off. Modular compounds, axis draughts, temporal variants. I'm done with the lot. I open my eyes and smile. "What a bore."

"Today's almost put me to sleep." Doctor Sabre motions towards the door and I follow, obediently. "Still, it has its uses." We head towards the staffroom, windows pointing the way. "This new curriculum is a killer."

"Headaches?"

"Not for me, some of my kids though. Two had to go without worms last week. I think their parents were pushing them too hard, they got frazzled. Poor bastards."

"It's a race; they don't want to be left behind."

The stench of the staff room hits us; a gorilla cage of stale sweat and acid breath. We print our caffeine and then recede to our usual corner. Some of the Physicals are stretching, some are competing to see who can outmanoeuvre the other's yoga stance. Doctor Abs is performing a one-handed handstand, her legs parted, feet rotating slowly, humming like a moron. Most of the Academics hover around the printer, filling themselves with sugars and caffeines, talking through the day's worm. The Head, a pompous, irritatingly articulate mound of muscle, is schmoozing. She doesn't like me.

"Okay, okay!" The Head whistles like we're a pack of dogs. "Over here! Settle down. Thank you."

I turn to Sabre and whisper, "Woof." She smiles and pretends to pant, her tongue lolling, before turning her attention to The Head.

"I've reviewed the recent results. Most are on target, but some are slipping. The High Ups aren't doing as well as we'd anticipated. Please, people, make sure you're sticking to the three D's: Data, Diet and…" The Head dangles the word like a fishing hook.

We all bite. "Diagnosis."

"Watch out, we have a duty of care here, people. Now, here's the latest from MediGov. Arms and legs inside the ride!" The Head laughs at her own lame joke, again. She pushes a button and Doctor Hello's bald, glinting blue head appears at the centre of the room.

"Dear Staff, MediGov have vital new information…"

I drown him out in a slurp of caffeine. Doctor Hello always has information to share, none of it vital. I look at Sabre, who catches my glance, smiles and nudges my arm, before her attentions return to Doctor Hello's updates. The Physicals are in ridiculous poses, balancing almost-impossibly on limbs and digits. Today's worm has finished absorbing, but my gut twists and stings like I've been shot in the stomach. I breathe slowly, sucking in a lung of sweaty air, and feel the bile rise in my throat. Gotta get out. I stand.

"You okay?" Sabre asks.

I whisper, not wanting to attract attention. "Yeh, just need air. Worm's down the wrong hole."

She smiles and I bolt to the door, heaving my breakfast onto the corridor floor. The kids will get a kick out of that, at least. I stare at the half-digested mounds of cereals and fruit tabs, frothing in my acids, until the Janitor arrives and instructs me to "Please vacate. Biohazard."

The Janitor sucks up my breakfast into him and trundles into a recharge port, I wipe my mouth just in time for the kids to return.

I have a free period before lunch, so walk to the computer labs, sit and pretend to work. Ads flash up for vacations I can't afford, clothes I hate the look of, content I dare not look at on school premises, discounts on worms.

LEARN ALL THE NEW WORLD LANGUAGES! 2 WORMS, 2 HOURS.

BECOME ONE WITH THE ANCIENT WORLD! THE COMPLETE WORKS OF SHAKESPEARE, WITH NOTES, IN JUST 1 WORM.

MILITARY STRATEGY. 1 WORM. BE THE BEST!

BOOKWORM! THE SKILLS SALE! HALF PRICE WORMS FOR ALL OUR SKILLS BOOKS! NOW INCLUDES MARTIAL ARTS FROM GRANDMASTERS, POETRY FROM THE POLARS, AND DATING FOR DUMMIES!

My finger twitches over the offers, but I close them and load my books. It's considered avant garde to read at the moment, something that only artists and time-wasters would bother with, but I still bother. I read before it was cool – that's what I tell the kids. They think it's pointless, and I agree sometimes. It would have taken years to learn the medical set, but the course of five worms (and a top up practical session) gave me enough knowledge to take this job. I can fix most things around the house if I need to, which saves me a bundle. I even learned how to gamble, but didn't have the knack for it. But taking a worm isn't the same as reading a book the old-fashioned way – something happens, I get involved. It's like walking around someone's house, checking out their photos, trying on their clothes, drinking their juice. The worm takes all of that away; it feels like you have the blueprints in your hands but never went inside for yourself. I miss the experience.

I swipe the screen and the page turns.

"Hey granddad." Sabre's hands rub my shoulders. I jerk, as if caught watching dodgy ads, and swipe the book away.

"Hey," I turn around, breaking her grip.

"You okay now? Saw the Janitor emptying the contents of your stomach into the flashbins."

"I'm fine, thanks. That Janitor's a blabbermouth."

"I'm just sneaky, that's all. So, you heard the news?"

"No, what?"

"New worms for the High Ups, and settlers to help with any side effects."

Waves of nausea rise and sink in me again. "How can we afford that?" There are cuts, always cuts, and worms are expensive. Giving the brighter kids extra worms and settlers will cost a fortune.

"Parents have to pay. Fifty-fifty expenses split with MediGov."

"Don't fancy the chances of the Low Downs, then."

"Me neither. Should we say something?"

Doctor Hello's cobalt head turns on the windows. He blinks at us. "Nah. They'll trial it, decide it's expensive and stop it. They always do."

"True." She shuffles. "Right, I've a task for you."

"Joy."

"You've got to take these to Sanctum School. The air's fine, so I'd go now."

"Says who?"

"Her headiness. The Head."

Damned Head. "What about class? I've got 2B this afternoon." My least favourite group, but I try to hide it.

Sabre sighs. "I'll take them. We've got to follow orders." She salutes jokingly. "Just pray that I make it out of 2B alive."

"You'll be fine." I grin, happy to be rid of them.

Sanctum School's across the city, but the weather's fine. I stroll, eager to take in as much sunlight as I can before the clouds return. Janitors suck up streaks of dust from the paths, wiping windows so that the ads are clear. The briefcase is lighter than it looks; reinforced alloy, photon-strapped to my wrist, packed with excess worms, a tiny ocean of them locked away. It would be less conspicuous without the strap but thefts are up lately, and the newscasters are eager to tell us about the dreaded reality of the world. "Stay In. Don't Take Risks. Watch Out For Deadheads." All the usual jargon we only half believe, and it's dissolved by a walk in the open air.

Sanctum's not too far but I don't fancy the Low Down side of town – too many Deadheads, too unpredictable. I run through the city maps I've memorised, checking the route. Heaven Park will take longer but it's scenic; I'll take it. I'm not eager to get back.

The park's brass gate welcomes me, its golden arches stretching high, gentle music willowing through the blades of grass and tree branches. A window reminds me to "Stick to the path (on pain of electrocution)" and I do. There are no Janitors, the floor and plants are already dusted clean, the stimulant birds tweet in their nests – *Four Seasons* by Vivaldi, I think, but I've not taken the Classical Music worm. They flutter their luminescent wings, scales glimmering like the real birds from the days before the clouds. I stand, close my eyes, lose myself in their song for a moment, before I fall to the floor.

"Get it! GET IT!"

"Shit, hurry!"

"Got it!"

The alarm is all I remember fully, and their faces. Two of them: one male, huge, muscular, deep black eyes, a sharp chin. The other: female, ruby red haired, green aug eyes. I tell the police everything I recall. They seem surprised.

"Not the usual suspects." The officer tells me, standing beside my hospital bed. "Unusual. What did they take?"

"Worms."

"Any particular kind?"

"I don't think so. Just educational ones, for high school."

"Thank you, you've been a great help. We'll find them. Sorry about your hand."

"Thanks."

Sabre enters as the cops leave, a look of sympathy on her face, holding a data card for the printer.

"Chocolates and grapes, I hope you like them." She inserts the data card and prints a small plate of dessert. "I'm not peeling them for you." She throws a grape into her mouth and chews, then forces a chocolate between my lips.

"Thanks."

"So, how's the hand? Did you get a good look at them?"

I pull the sheet from my mound of flesh, where my hand is being rebuilt. "Fine, it takes a week they said. Recycled nanites, but I'll be back to normal."

"A week off, nice. All doped up?"

"Yeh, pretty sweet. And yes, I saw them. It was over quickly though, they just cut through me and took the briefcase. Left me on the damned grass, buzzing."

"Ouch! Well, you'll be fine. We really need to do something about all the Deadheads though, it's getting too much. Normal people are getting hurt. I'm not going near that park again, not alone anyway."

"Me neither. And those martial arts worms, whatever they were, didn't help a bit, I didn't even see the attack coming."

"Waste of money." Sabre offers me another chocolate, I refuse, and she chomps it down. "Anyway I just came to check you're okay. And to give you this in person." She swipes at the window and a Get Well Soon card appears: the staff and some students are smiling, with Doctor Hello at the centre. "I added Hello, I know how much you love and admire him."

"Yeh, thanks for that." I pull a face, part playful and part genuinely disgruntled. "He's my hero."

Sabre doesn't come back to the hospital and the week drags. The thought of going back to the school – to the insipid jargon of Doctor Hello, the sweat-laden staff, the smarmy kids, the hours of boredom, the worms, everything except for Sabre – fills me with jitters, so I take meds to ease my nerves. I spend my wages on printer data, some new games, a few dozen books, put a couple of worms on order, cancel them. I watch the rolling news: crisis in the far West, politicians bickering, education at the centre of most stories.

"The divide between rich and poor," the broadcaster says, "is epidemic." He visits a worm farm, a vast glimmering factory full of flashing glass tanks. He dips his gloved hand into a tank and pulls out a handful of worms, shows how they flinch at bright lights.

"It's learned from their ancestors," he says to the camera. We know the story by now, but he tells it anyway. History repeats. "These worms never experienced light and shock therapy, yet they react to it. The reflex memory is passed on through the chemicals of other worms' experiences." The camera cuts to the human labs. "This lab collects data from these great minds." Rows of men and women sit, reading books and data sheets, swiping windows, listening to music through headphones. "All this, to make worms. But some feel that the big question still needs answers: are worms really good for us? Only time will tell."

I turn the news off, pack my bags and stretch the fingers of my new hand. No scars, the kids will be disappointed. I'm a little disappointed, too. Everyone likes a scar, it's a story lived and worth remembering.

Russell Jones is an Edinburgh-based writer and editor. He has published 4 collections of poetry, and has edited 2 poetry anthologies. He is the deputy and poetry editor of *Shoreline of Infinity* and writes SFF novels for young adults.

Whimper

Nalo Hopkinson

Da-da-de-dum the light burning within,
Because this cherry world is brighter than sin.

She ran and ran through the undark nightlit city, crashing past parked cars and motorbikes, shoving between two raucous, dressed-to-pussfoot women waiting in the line to get into Dutty Wine. They yelled hey and wha de rass as she broke through them. Smell of orange blossom shampoo and musk perfume from the two of them glazed the inside of her nose. Screams from the Dutty Wine line as her leggobeast ploughed through it, questing tirelessly for her. She sped away from the sound. The sea was so close. Down that alley. She careened in that direction.

Her right footfront jammed up against something hard. Bright pain blossomed in her toes. Probably a flagstone jooking up out of the sidewalk. She couldn't take time to look down. She staggered in her purple plimsolls. Right knee made a crunk sound, collapsed a little outwards. She felt the dislocation but not the pain from it. Made shift to stay on her feet, to runrunrun. Metallic quadruple thumps following behind her, repeated. She had to reach to the sea wall, throw herself over the side. The air she sucked in sandpapered her throat, debrided her lungs. Her heart in her chest was a boiling kettle. Her open mouth the whistle. She pushed on down the alleyway. Crumpled right knee now stabbing knives into her kneecap with every stride.

Leggobeasts-them couldn't abide sea water. People said so. Don' know which people, after nobody survived the touch of their leggobeast. Every hour of day nor night nowadays, the harbour full up of desperate bodies, only their heads showing as they bobbed on the oily water. Leggobeasts waited patiently at the water's edge until the person they were chasing gave up and swam back to them to be taken, or got too exhausted to swim and gave their lungs to the water. But she wouldn't. She wouldn't. If she could only reach before the leggobeast touched her.

She clattered through the alley, sobbing. Stumbled around a discarded mattress that reeked heavy of man piss. Sloshed through a reddish muddy liquid that smelled worse. Broken bottles crunched underfoot. And behind her, maybe only couple-three yards now, her personal leggobeast. Everybody had one. At least, is so people said. And when your time come, it going to get you, no matter what. Hers was an iron donkey. And tonight was her time. Her knee screamed with each step. But she moved. The clanking clatter sounded closer. Two yards? One? Her throat-hole was on fire. She broke out of the alleyway, hooves thumpity thump behind her, near enough to throw the shadow of an equine muzzle over her shoulder and onto the ground. Flat, dark sea in front of her, across the two-lane highway. Only things between her and the water: light traffic and the low metal restraining wall. Ranged out all along the narrow lip of soil between the sea wall and the sea; silhouettes of leggobeasts. Each one different.

No time. People had it to say that only the touch of your personal leggobeast would kill you; you were safe from all the others. She dodged cars, blowing panic and pain through her lips. Threw herself over the side of the restraining wall. Limped to the edge. Pushed between two of the shadows. One had deep, rough fur and rank breath. They breathed? The other felt like tree bark.

She let herself fall into the water. A floret of bubbles bloomed upwards around her as she plunged down. She stroked, pushing for the air above. She tried to kick, but her knee screamed at her. She broke the surface and kept swimming away from the shoreline as quickly as she could. She wasn't a good swimmer. The water might as well have been molasses.

"Ow!"

Her hand had smacked someone in the head.

"Sorry," she hissed through clenched teeth. "Beg pardon."

"Is all right," the other woman replied. "Just go easy. Plenty of we in here."

Treading water – though not with the bad leg – she looked around. Her sight had adjusted to the dark. Yes, heads bobbing everywhere, all of them staring back at their leggobeasts on the shore. She swivelled herself around in the water to face hers. "Why nobody swimming away?" she asked the woman beside her.

"Swimming to go where?"

She hadn't thought it through that far. "To a ship?" The harbour was strangely empty.

A man not too far off said, "Once you on the ship, you not in water any more. Your leggobeast will just materialize and take you." His voice was hoarse.

"How long you been in the water?" Sea salt was already making her lips pucker.

He replied, "I don't know. Maybe two days? I can't hold on a lot longer."

Voices called out from the darkness: one day; one hour; don't remember how long; so hungry. A man with bloodshot eyes said, "My own show up this afternoon. Been waiting for 'im. I throw two good bullets in 'im rass from my gun. The shots land, but the bullet holes close right over."

The woman she'd bumped into – who was now dog-paddling slow circles around her – asked, "Which one is yours?" She jutted her chin towards the shore line.

"The shiny one." Her leggobeast had taken its place in the line-up. It was perched, delicately as a hill-climbing goat, on the shallow ledge of land. It looked at her, she was sure of it. It stamped one foot. The air and water were so still, she could hear its bolts rattle.

The woman said, "Look my own yah-so. Three over from yours, to the right."

"The one that look like a tree?"

"A cashew tree, in fact. With a child's face embedded in the trunk."

Something touched her shoulder. She jerked away from it and yelled out before she saw what it was. A length of wooden plank, not yet waterlogged. She grabbed it, gratefully let it take some of her weight. She called out, "I find a piece of wood. Allyuh want to share?"

"Yes, please, lady, do!"

"And me!"

Pretty soon, five of the floaters were clinging to the length of branch, with the rest holding onto their ankles. Had been six of them, but one of them had disappeared as soon as he touched the wood. On the shore, the structure that had looked like a crumbling old shack had disappeared at the same time. She'd forgotten; that was a leggobeast, too.

Soon they had a third row of people clinging to the people clinging to the five. They all starfished out on the surface of the water. She said to the woman who'd first spoken to her, "How come the plank didn't disappear when the leggobeast took that guy?"

"Don't know. I really have to pee."

The water between her and the woman got warm for a few seconds, then cooled off again.

"Sorry."

"Don't fret."

They all floated in silence for awhile. From the horizon, a wash of blue was creeping up the sky. On the shore, her iron donkey reared. It thrust its muzzle to the sky, came down with a clank and a rattling of bolts.

"Yours talk to you?" the young woman asked.

"Only in my dreams."

"I used to dream about mine, too. That's how I knew it was coming."

She called out, more to make conversation than because she really wanted to know, "Allyuh not thirsty? And how you shit?"

"We do it right ya so, lady. The sea does carry it away."

The sea salt was burning her lips. She started to moisten them with her tongue. Thought of what she was floating in. Spat instead. She didn't have plenty to spit with; her mouth was nearly dry. "And how you eat?"

"We don't..."

"I see one boy. He get tired waiting for death. He swim right back up to his leggobeast. Grabbed its ankle. It took him."

She said, "You know what I wonder?"

Someone replied, "What?"

"How we so sure is a bad thing for our leggobeastst to fetch us away?"

"How you mean, how? Is obvious, nuh?"

"No, think; maybe they take us to something better than this. Well, of course better than this right here. But I mean, your lives before your leggobeast; what those were like?"

Thereafter came a litany of joys and woes: a good job; a dying husband; a call from a long lost friend; fifty dollars found between the couch cushions; poverty; prosperity; failed exams; cancer diagnoses. And the guy who admitted having just shot his best friend. The rest of them edged away from him, spoiling the symmetry of the starfish. He sobbed. They watched. Snot glistened on his upper lip. He wailed, "I so sorry, Robbie!" The sobs crested, then fell off. The man let go his hold on the person who was supporting him and floated, spinning in a slow circle. No-one moved to stop him. On the shore, a gelid lump, man-high, disappeared. So did the murderer's body. She couldn't see how he had died.

"See?" said the woman, her new friend in adversity. "That's how we know is a bad thing to let your leggobeast catch you. Even if they don't touch you, when you dead, they go, too. So they nuh must mean death?"

"And that's a bad thing?" The gonging pain in her knee was almost background noise, a spike being driven over and over again into her cold-numbed leg. One of the starfish arms was holding that ankle, but she barely noticed.

"So," said the young woman. "You didn't answer your own question."

She went silent. She didn't want to do this.

But the woman persisted. "What your life was like? Something to stay for, or to run from?"

She swallowed. "I running from the end of the world."

"Of course is the end. One of those things for every human on the planet. How running going to help?"

"I need to stop it. Cause is me who start it."

Murmurs from around and behind her. A voice said, "You? How you coulda do this?"

Someone else said, "Is not she. Is aliens."

Someone else ventured, "Messengers of God."

She said, "No. Is me. I dream them."

The youth across from her: "We all dream them. Is that make we know we number come up."

She replied, "I dream all of them. Every single one. Before this ever start. Dream them by the score. Dream armies of them. I still dreaming them. Six billion of them is a lot of dreaming."

No-one said anything. The sky had lightened to fore-day morning; enough for her to make out their stunned expressions. She pointed to the shore. "That one there? With all those foot-long teeth? I dream he last year. Looking exactly so. I dream the one that take away the Prime Minister last month." She pointed farther down the line. "That one that could be a little girl in her frilly princess dress, except she have too many legs? I dream she. The bruk-down house this plank come from? I dream it last night. Same time I dream my own."

Someone made a small, sad noise. "That duppy girl with the plenty foot is my one. You really send that thing after me? You send them after alla we?"

The creatures were starting to shuffle and shift about uneasily where they stood. Oh, god. She knew what was coming. "I didn't do it on purpose!" she yelled. "I tried to stop! But how you going to hold back your dreams?"

"I know a way," said a voice. A hand gripped the back of her neck and shoved her beneath the water. She stopped up her breath and struggled, but the hand was too strong. There was commotion all around her; legs kicking. Were they trying to help her, or to help drown her? She wished she could stop fighting, let herself die. Had been wishing it since this all started.

The implacable hand was still holding her down. Her lungs bellowed, airless. From underneath, the surface of the water was a refractive lens. It let her see all the leggobeasts in their long line at the edge of the sea. Spots floated in front of her eyes. She tried to stop struggling, but her body wouldn't give up. Her mind, though, was thinking quickquickquick. Do it quick. Because last night, her dreams had changed. The leggobeasts had changed. Even as she couldn't hold her breath any longer, opened her mouth and sucked killing brine into herself, she watched the leggobeasts.

Together, moving as one, they floated a few feet up into the air. As she twisted and drowned, she saw the leggobeasts, each flying towards their person. Her iron donkey was in the air above her, starting to descend towards her. She hadn't told the young woman, she remembered. Hadn't told her what the iron donkey said to her in her dre

Nalo Hopkinson is a yardie by birth, a Canuck by citizenship, and a child of literary parents. In her brain, language dances and dance is a language. She creates weird things, including fiction and mermaids. She has won the World Fantasy and Andre Norton Awards. She's a professor of Creative Writing at the University of California Riverside, where she's a member of a research cluster in science fiction. This story was written for the final issue of Black Clock journal, in which all the stories were named either "Bang" or "Whimper," and all ended in the middle of a sente

www.nalohopkinson.com
www.patreon.com/nalo_hopkinson

First published in Shoreline of Infinity 3 - winner of our first short story competition

The Great Golden Fish

Dee Raspin

Art: Stephen Pickering

Angus sat on a rough stone, overlooking the glen where his croft lay. Propping his crook by his side, he raised his eyes to the shifting storm clouds, and sighed. The croft had lost its heart since Mary died. He couldn't bear to sit at the big table alone, with nothing but the crackle of logs on the fire to break the silence.

With Mary there was never silence, rest, or peace. There was always something needing doing. Dying wool, carding it, spinning it, knitting it, making him wear it – though it never fit. Or she'd be out in the fields, tilling the earth with all the pull of a barrel-backed pony. She was a strong lass, Mary.

The first time they'd met at old Campbell's cèilidh, that's what he'd noticed: her strength. It shone in her broad, fearless smile, in the red of her cheeks, in the dark glitter of her eyes. When she danced, there was something wild in her movements.

Angus had been fine-looking in his youth, and all the lassies blushed and giggled when he walked by.

All but one – and she was hurling the menfolk about like hayricks, as she raced through the dance.

There was a woman who could work! Angus wasn't for wanting a fireside decoration. He wasn't for cow-like docility, good manners and old-fashioned respect. He propped himself against the barn wall, waiting to catch her eye. One by one, she left her partners exhausted. Even Rob Mackay, the big miller's son, was starting to slow. But not Mary – the more she spun, stomped and reeled, the brighter her eyes grew and the redder her cheeks.

She looked up, and locked eyes with Angus.

It wasn't an invitation to dance, it was a challenge to battle – and he knew it. Throwing back her head, black ringlets falling around her neck and shoulders, she took him by the hand and pulled him to the floor. The men roared with laughter, the women rolled their eyes.

Surely bonny Angus wasn't after big Mary?

The rest of the night he and she danced every dance together. They twisted each other's arms, trampled each other's feet and laughed loud enough to drown out the band.

Hours later, when the dance ended, they headed out into the hills in search of the sunrise. Their breath fell heavy on the chill air, and the little clouds of mist they made mingled together. When they reached the big cairn, they sat down – gazing into the distance. There the world stretched out before them – golden, bathed in the first light of morning. Everything fresh, and new.

Angus turned to Mary, and she met his glance with a steady eye and firm smile.

"Mary." he said, and she knew what he was about. "If yer as brutal with my cows as yer are wi' me, ye'll be my ruin."

And that was that. They married the following month.

Not long after, Angus saw a new side to the wild lass. With animals, she was calm – yet stern. There was a depth in her that seemed to soothe them. Even the stags in season would cease their bellowing for Mary. The years Angus shared with her were happy and quick.

But then, one winter, sad news came drifting down into the glen. They heard of folk turned out of their crofts, without a stitch, forced to make way for sheep. The sheep made more money than the crofters paid rent, they said. It was called "The Clearances."

But what of the people? They were sent to the coast, to fish.

To fish! Men and women that'd never seen the sea.

Angus shivered.

But there was more to come. Mary's father was ill. He'd had news of a close friend's death, and taken it badly. Mary's father and Hamish Mackenzie had been friends for years. Even when

Mary's father moved down into the glen, Hamish would send messages by travelling men with news and talk.

It was a dark afternoon when the messenger came knocking. His face was grave, his eyes downcast. The men had come, chasing folks out their houses. But old Hamish was stubborn – he'd refused to leave. More than that, he'd grown frail. How could he, at his age, make a journey to the coast and start afresh? How could he learn to fish; a man who'd worked the fields all his life?

When they threatened him, he laughed in their faces. Better die here, in his boyhood home, than some godforsaken coast.

And die, he did.

That night they came and set his croft alight – with Hamish inside. His screams echoed through the hills, but there was no help to be had: the place went up so fast.

Mary tried to console her father, but it was useless – he lay in bed, unresponsive. His eyes were clouded with thoughts of another place, and he saw and heard nothing. Day after day, he grew thinner. A week later, he died. The grief had been too much.

And as is often the case with sorrow, it spread like disease.

Mary, the woman who'd never known illness, started to grow pale.

At first Angus didn't notice. Then, he wouldn't notice. It didn't make sense. Illness was for other people. Mary was constant, like the hills: something time passed by, not something it changed. She was strong, like the rocks – nothing could bend her.

But, soon, Angus had to accept his mistake – Mary was mortal. He saw the difference in her eyes. They'd grown dark, and the light had left. Now she would sit by the fire, staring into the flames for hours on end – hands by her side, empty. If it weren't for Angus, the cows would have gone unfed and the crops untended.

The extra work didn't bother him. Mary bothered him. To see her as she was now – so close by his side, but so far from him in her mind – tore him up. She seldom spoke. And when she did, she talked of strange fanciful stuff – and that was worse. She didn't ask after the cows, tell him to fetch firewood, or sweep the

floor. Now, with her eyes lifted to the skies, she would babble of
fish.

"The fish, Angus." she would say. "It's coming. I can see it"
and she would clench her fists, and smile. "It's getting nearer, it's
getting closer."

He would pull a seat up by her side, pat her back in a way he'd
seen other men pet their wives, and ask what she meant.

"A flying fish." she would whisper. "It's coming through the
skies, with a ladder to escape."

And Angus would withdraw his hand from her back, head out
onto the hills, and try to clear his mind. Try to understand how
this could have happened to Mary. Try to understand when all
this madness and sorrow had started. In truth, something in her
words made his skin prickle. She spoke with such conviction.
Her tone, so calm. To her, this madness was truth. She absolutely
believed a flying fish was coming to save them.

And then, when he was sure he was alone, he would cry.

A few days later, Mary grew worse. All day she spoke of her
father, golden fish, iron discs and strange singing.

Angus never strayed from her side. Hour by hour, he watched
her fade. After all these years, she was leaving him.

When night fell, she grew silent – watching the moon. And
when morning came, she watched the sun. He tried to make her
look away, but she would not. Her eyes grew red and sore.

Around midday, with a faint smile and a sigh, she died.

That afternoon Angus sat on the rock, gazing down at the glen.
There was nothing, now Mary was gone.

Weeks passed. Every day found Angus seated on the rock,
staring at the sky. All day he sat watching the shifting clouds,
whispering "A fish, Mary? A fish?"

He grew thin, and so did his cows. But there was a spark in his
eye that hadn't been there before. It might have been madness.

Then the news came, again – the Clearances were coming.

It was around this time Mary began speaking to him at night.
The voice didn't sound like Mary's – it was unearthly, metallic and
distant. But, like a dream where one thing represents another,

Angus knew it was his wife. "Ach, you're slow! Tsk, tsk" she'd mock, with a laugh. And Angus would speed up whatever task he was about, but it made no difference. A tingle would run down his spine and the words "God, man! Are you no done yet?" would ring in the air. What he wasn't doing fast enough for her liking, he couldn't guess – she never told him.

Sometimes, she'd just sing. And the sound would thrum through his bones and into his brain. Then, at night, he would dream of strange iron discs, men and women with shining faces, and a golden place far beyond the clouds.

But the voice never caused him terror. It was just Mary. If there was a body who'd not be put off by death, it was Mary. Interfering from the afterlife? Aye, no surprises there.

One night she spoke to him louder than ever. "Wake up, Angus! They're coming." Her voice cracked down his spine like a whip. "Leave, leave!"

He sat up in bed, his brain still fogged with sleep. "What? And go where?"

"The tree by the cairn." she answered, her voice sharp and quick – like it used to be when they were chopping timber, and he wasn't working fast enough. "Wait there 'til morning, and dinnae stir!"

He got up. Somewhere in the distance he could hear men's cries. He didn't look back, but headed straight for the cairn.

He'd always told her she had eyes like a witch. They were so dark and wild. They seemed to know secrets stolen from another world.

Angus waited on the hillside, stopping his ears with his fingers, watching as fires sprang up in the glen.

Moment by moment, they grew closer.

At last, a few men drew up to the croft. He watched as they banged on the door. They waited a few minutes, before breaking it down and stepping inside. Then they were out again, empty handed. With a shrug, a thin man threw a lit torch towards the thatch.

The weather'd been dry these last few days, and the flames leapt up.

Angus watched, numb.

After a while, a feeling started in his chest. He couldn't describe it. There in the pre-dawn darkness, it grew with the flames. It tugged through his body, like briar thorns and nettle stings. It wound tighter and tighter, until his chest ached and he vomited.

To lose everything at once – it seemed impossible. To spend so much time building so much – to lose it all so fast. The world was mad. He was mad – widowed, speaking to his dead wife through dreams, watching their house burn to nothing.

What was he? Who was Angus MacDonald? That man had a wife, a house, livestock.

The man's body he was in now had none of those things. He was a bundle of nerves, drenched in vomit, cold in the night.

Morning came. He didn't remember falling asleep. It must have been exhaustion.

The ruin of his home lay before him. There it was – just a frame and stones. The soul had burned away. Little silver grey wisps of smoke curled up from the last few glowing embers. He imagined the soul of his home going to greet the afterlife.

"Farewell," he sighed, his voice hollow. There was nothing to feel. His loss was so complete – he was no one. Even his emotions were gone. They'd taken them, too – when they killed his Mary and set his life on fire.

But the sensation, deep in his chest, was strengthening. It throbbed in the darkness inside him. It was heavy, dull and colourless. And as he sat, it grew. He felt it spreading out – like a tree, with branches thorned with ice. Hour after hour, it kept growing.

After a time, Angus realised what it meant.

Death. He wanted death to come down and take him away.

He lay on the earth, watching the sky. Hour after hour, the clouds shifted above. He felt nothing, but the prickling branches of the tree as it continued to grow.

Darkness faded the sky. He watched as sunset painted the clouds a beautiful blood red. He felt no need for food, he could live off those colours – the colours the heavens sent. He drank them deep, pulling them inside. He felt the tree stop growing, but it didn't fade. It stayed.

The sky flecked a thousand different colours, growing more and more beautiful. How had he never noticed this miracle before? His eyes had always been bent to the earth; too busy toiling for himself to notice the glory of a sunset.

Night came, and the tree started growing again. Its roots filled his stomach; staving off hunger. Its branches crawled upwards, till they clutched his throat, and tightened there. The pain went beyond tears.

Somewhere in the distance came the drumming of a snipe. The bird's weird trilling filled the air with an unearthly quality and Angus found his mind wandering to strange places. He dreamt of fairies, ghosts, water horses, witches and demons. He thought of all the children that went missing, and were never heard of again. If anything unholy existed, it would find him tonight.

Morning came, and with it nothing.

"Where do the dead go when they die? For them no world, but empty sky," whispered the tree in his chest.

How many days had passed since he last ate? He didn't know. But, he hadn't grown thinner. He wasn't hungry. Eating didn't seem like something he needed to do.

Night was coming, again.

Then, he heard it: a strange, distant creaking. A breeze stirred the grass by his side. Angus listened for the sound. Steadily, it grew louder. Every now and then a soft creak and distant whir floated to him on the air. It reminded him of the heave of the plough, but stretched out further.

The sound came louder and closer than before. Now it was like the strain of a saddle on a pony's back.

In the twilight, he saw it. There between the clouds came a strange thing. It was long and pointed – like the ships gypsies talked of. But, above the ship, there glowed a great fish. It was crafted from sticks, covered in leather, and painted with gold.

He gazed around the glen, at the rubble. There was only silence. Even the birds were quiet.

As the ship came closer he noticed something – the clouds hadn't moved since its arrival. They lay in the sky – static. The ship passed through, without disturbing them. An odd feeling stirred in his heart. Everything was absolutely still. No winds moved the leaves on the trees. It was as if the world had died.

A low, clanking, metallic sound thrummed through the glen, as the ship came closer. The fish twisted this way and that, controlling the ship with each movement. And, as he listened closer, the sounds became music. It was the dark, enchanting song of another world – all soft grinding iron and rhythmic clanging.

For a moment his mind wandered to the devil and sorcery. But the ship was something different altogether – there were no spirits at work here, evil or otherwise. The whole world was calm. His body didn't ache. He wasn't tired.

The ship came to rest above the hilltop tree, a few feet away. Then, he saw it – a strange figure; tall and glinting in the light of the moon. As it turned to face him, his stomach tightened. It was a man, made from metal – with a metal beard, and a metal hat. The detail – the workmanship – was astounding. It was as if a real man had been set in gold, and jointed to allow movement. In the darkness, the thing's eyes glowed faint green.

It lowered a ladder to the ground, and started climbing down from the ship. Its movements were gliding and seamless, but each came to an abrupt, jittering halt.

Angus searched for the terror he should feel, but there was none. Only interest.

He waited as the thing strode across the earth, coming to meet him.

When it was a few paces away, it stopped, opened its mouth, and spoke.

"Evening, Angus."

The words sounded like they'd been dragged up from the depths of a huge copper basin.

Angus hesitated, unable to respond.

The thing cocked its head. "Mister MacDonald, it's time to leave."

Before Angus could think, he found himself following the metal man to the ladder – as if hypnotised.

The ship seemed ancient. The timber was dark and weathered, worn smooth with polish. Metal handles stuck out from the wood. They were golden, covered in intricate detail – worn so much as to be unintelligible. And at the front of the ship, circles of toothed iron interlocked and spun around; creating the song he'd heard before. Now he could hear undercurrents of smaller metal circles, creating an additional jangle.

High above, the sky stretched out – sprinkled with stars, glittering like ice shards. He'd never seen a sky like this. The dark blue was woven with purple, and the clouds seemed like spun silver. Everything was a dream.

There should be so many questions to ask, but his mind was blank. Only his eyes and ears were awake.

The metal man began to sing, and his voice blended with the moving iron circles, until it sounded like the world was dancing away into the night.

When Angus woke, the sky was bright blue, and golden clouds flocked above. The ship was still sailing through the air, but the metal man was quiet now – staring straight ahead.

Angus followed his gaze.

There in front, lay a strange sight. A raft of golden crofts hung suspended from golden fish. Together they formed a settlement. Between them lay pavements of bright shining metal.

The metal man docked the ship next to a small croft, and helped Angus down the ladder, onto the street. They walked through street after street. Soon, Angus noticed the crofts were getting bigger. After a while, they came across crofts with two floors – one above the other. Later, these gave way to crofts with three floors, then four, and so on. Eventually, the golden buildings reached up so high, there was nothing to see but brick on either side. The sky was nothing but a mass of golden fish, all crowded together.

Here it was warm, and the air was infused with the smell of oil. The thrum of grinding iron shivered in the background, making music.

The streets were filled with men and women, all of them metallic and glistening.

As they walked deeper and deeper into the golden mass, Angus realised the music was of all the dances he'd ever danced – woven into one. Then, in the midst of it, he caught a voice – singing in beat. It was low, murmuring, echoing and metallic – yet higher pitched than the metal man's. It pulsed, pulling them onward.

Soon, Angus realised it was a heartbeat – filling everything with movement and binding it all together.

Its accent was foreign, yet familiar. So familiar.

It rang in his ears.

As they walked further, golden cows jostled amongst the golden men and golden women.

At last they reached an enormous croft. Cows crowded the entrance, and herbs, fish and meat hung in the windows.

Here, the music was clearest.

The metal man pushed the door open.

Inside, the croft was flooded with water. It was warm, and it reached past their ankles. In it swarmed hundreds of small golden fish, flicking their tails and circling together. From the ceiling hung fishing nets, strewn with golden seaweed and glittering shells.

Questions filled Angus's mind, but the singing filled the place so completely there seemed no room for his words.

Together, he and the metal man passed through room after room. The place reminded him of a honeycomb – so many tiny interlocking rooms. They were in the centre of a hive.

There before them rose a great chair, and behind it burned an enormous fire in a hearth shaped like a fish's mouth.

In the chair sat a golden woman. Angus felt his heart freeze in his chest as he looked at her.

Her wild hair hung down to her shoulders. Like the rest of her, it was cast from gold. Her eyes glowed faint blue. And, in her right hand, she held a crook – like a sceptre.

"Mary!" he cried, recognition flooding his senses.

"Aye, Angus." she said, with a mechanical smile, followed by a metallic laugh. "Welcome home."

"Home?" The word had never sounded so alien.

"Aye, home." She nodded to the golden fish circling about his feet. "You're no home yet, though. No while there's still soil on your heels."

He looked down. His feet were brown with dirt, and the toenails had grown long, dark and twisted.

"Aye," she sighed. "You're no aging well. Life's going by fast."

Climbing down from her seat, she went to meet him – taking him by the hand.

Together, they walked through vast, glittering corridors. They went on further and further through the maze.

At last, they came to a huge, dark hall. In the centre, a great glowing fish floated in the air. From its mouth came the song of everything.

Angus felt a hand on his back as Mary gave him a push.

"Dance. Dance with him, Angus."

Angus stumbled forward, his mind blurred. The fish turned its great dazzling eyes upon him. They were blue as summer sky, flecked with dark blue spots of velvet night.

"Dance," Mary whispered.

Angus stepped closer, and the fish began to move. First it swayed its head, then its fins, then its tail. Then all parts of the great golden fish were in motion. Angus felt his feet gliding this way and that through the water, beating time. The fish drew closer, until their bodies were touching. Together they twisted and turned through a dance so intricate it could never be learnt. Yet Angus knew it. He felt it flowing up from somewhere deep inside. As they moved, Angus realised the fish's scales were staining his skin. Wherever they touched, they left golden metallic patches.

The dance went on and on. It must have lasted days, but there was no way of knowing. He never tired, and Mary stood, silent – watching. He saw his toenails shrink back to normal, and the dirt on his feet melt away. The more he danced, the less tired he got. His chest grew clear, and his breathing came easier than ever. At last, the fish withdrew, and swam away – high up into the blackness of the towering ceiling.

Mary stepped forward, taking his hand. "Aye, now it's done, my bonny golden laddie."

Angus saw his reflection in the rippling water. His face and hair were golden, and his eyes glowed a quiet blue.

He turned to her, and smiled.

Dee Raspin hails from a small town on the north-east coast of the Scottish Highlands. A Creative Writing graduate of Napier University, she takes inspiration from steampunk, Scottish history and mythology. Her work has been described as 'psychedelic folk'. If cornered, she will likely claim to be working on a novel. The details of said novel remain suspiciously obscure. She is honoured to be part of Scotland's only sci-fi magazine, *Shoreline of Infinity*.

First published in Shoreline of Infinity 4

Senseless

Gary Gibson

Art: Dave Alexander

Bill tasted the sweet, sharp scent of violence in the back of his throat just a moment before the fight broke out – although calling it a *fight* was stretching it, given O'Hare was a notorious sociopathic from Hut Thirteen and Ade, the object of his ire, was a skinny little guy on crutches who could hardly stand straight, let alone defend himself.

Bill heard O'Hare's guttural roar as he grabbed hold of Ade and sent him tumbling to the canteen floor, his crutches clattering down beside him. Bill reacted without thinking. He threw his tin tray to one side and shoved O'Hare in the back as hard as he could with both hands. O'Hare lost his balance, his cheap prison-issue boots performing a complicated shuffle as he tried to stay upright. He collided with a kitchen trolley, sending dishes scattering across the tiles with a noise like cymbals thrown down a stairwell.

A whistle shrieked, cutting through the yells of the other prisoners. Guards seized hold of Bill, twisting his arms behind his back and dragging him out into the freezing autumn air. They came to a halt and he listened as they unlocked a door before shoving him inside.

He sprawled on icy concrete, listening as the guards locked the door again before retreating back across the compound.

He waited there, shivering and hungry, for three days before another guard brought him a bowl of hot broth that sank down his throat like a tiny burning star. He'd barely had time to taste it before his wrists were cuffed behind his back and he was led back across the prison compound and inside the main building, recognisable by its distinctive echoes. There he waited, the guard's hand never leaving his shoulder, until a buzzer sounded and he was led through a door.

"You're new," he said, standing at the threshold of the interrogation room.

"How do you know?" The woman's voice had a slight Scottish lilt to it. "It says in your records that you're blind, Mister Sharpe."

"I…" Bill realised he'd slipped badly. Hunger and cold would do that to you. "I just guessed."

The truth was that Bill knew everyone in the camp by their scent, and hers was unfamiliar, burdened as it was by the unusually rich perfume of the soap she had used that morning.

The guard pushed Bill into a chair. He sat clumsily. He could sense, but not see, the desk before him, and the woman sitting behind it. He pictured her as having very white skin, with narrow lips and red hair pulled back in a tight bun above a National Unity uniform.

"My name is Hannegan," she said. "I'm with the Office of Investigations. And you're correct – I am new. So why don't we start with you telling me why you attacked Mister O'Hare the other day?"

"He attacked Ade – I share a hut with him. Ade has to use crutches. It's a struggle for him to stay upright or even hold onto a tray. I usually help him, but O'Hare pushed between us in line when we got there that morning. I guess he got tired of waiting for Ade to collect his morning ration."

"Who is this Ade?"

"Adebayo," said Bill.

"Ah." Bill heard the sound of a pencil pressed against paper. "Adebayo Afolayan. An African. Another Senseless."

"He's from Leeds, not Africa."

The guard, still standing behind him, cuffed Bill across the back of the head. "Don't try and be smart."

"And that was reason enough for you to attack Mister O'Hare?" Hannegan pressed.

"Ade is on *crutches*," said Bill. "How the hell was he going to defend himself? He's disabled!"

"Yes, but no one is disabled unless they choose to be," the woman pointed out.

"It's not his choice to—" Bill managed to stop himself before the rest of the words slipped out.

Fingers tapped on a desktop. "But it *is* his choice," Hannegan continued, with more than a hint of satisfaction. "The same as it's your choice to be blind. Give us even just one name, and I'll have you taken to the clinic right now and have your eyesight restored." He heard her chair creak beneath her. "According to these records, you've held out on us for two years. I'd almost think, Mister Sharpe, that you *like* being blind. You can go now."

The guard pulled Bill up and out of his seat before leading him back across the room.

"Oh, and if you don't mind me asking," said Hannegan, just before the guard pulled the door open again, "how did you know Mister O'Hare attacked your friend, and not someone else?"

Bill didn't turn around. "I didn't. Someone told me after the fact."

"Who, Mister Sharpe? You were immediately placed in solitary for several days. There's no one who could have told you."

Bill shrugged, working to make the gesture look casual. "I guess someone shouted his name."

On the way back out, Bill caught Ade's scent, and guessed he was next to be interviewed. The guard led him back out past the canteen building, then further uphill to the shale-roofed wooden hut that had been his home on the island for the last hundred weeks. As soon as he was inside and the guard was gone, he felt Owen's fingers pressing against his bare forearm, tracing out letters.

Big problem, wrote Owen. *Someone new coming.*

"I know," Bill said, turning to where he knew Owen was. They'd made Owen deaf as well as mute, but he'd learned to be an efficient lipreader. "I just met her. Hannegan. She must be the new interrogator."

Owen shook Bill's arm violently. *No*, he wrote. *Another Senseless. Tonight.*

The words brought Bill a jolt of alarm. "In our hut?"

Yes, Owen drew, his scent heavy with fear. *Change plans?*

Bill licked his lips, scenting even his own fear. "I don't know," he said. "Does Ade know about this?"

Yes.

Well, that was something, anyway. Ade could at least speak, even if they'd taken away his sense of proprioception.

"Wait until Ade's back," said Bill. "Then we'll talk more."

Ade returned an hour later, stumbling like a drunkard even with the aid of his crutches. Bill listened to the sound of his carefully measured movements as he made his way across the hut. He'd been a concert pianist before his arrest, but nowadays he'd be lucky to sit on a piano stool without sliding straight off.

"There you are," said Ade, falling into a chair by the hut's single table. He leaned back, anchoring himself to the back of the chair by hooking his arms over it, his legs sprawled before him at an awkward angle. "I saw you back there."

Bill nodded. "You spoke with that new interrogator?"

"She's been talking to all the Senseless prisoners, it seems."

"What does she look like?" Bill asked suddenly.

"Why don't you tell me?"

"Red hair, pale skin? Hair in a bun?"

Ade laughed with delight. "How the hell do you always *know*?"

A long time ago – before the plagues, the crop failures, the toxic algal blooms killing the oceans and the concomitant collapse in social order – Bill had read about something called blindsight. In certain circumstances, if their optic nerves weren't damaged, the blind could see – after a fashion. Even though the visual data wasn't reaching the conscious part of their brain, they were nonetheless aware of their surroundings on an unconscious level, precisely as if they remained sighted. Somehow, Bill didn't need to see Hannegan's face to know what she looked like: on some deep-wired level he just *knew*.

Bill shrugged. "Owen said there's someone coming to stay with us?"

"We got the news while you were locked up."

"We only have three bunks in here. There's no room"

"Does it matter?" Ade's scent was heavy with anxiety. "We're supposed to be escaping from this miserable shithole – how are we going to do that with somebody new in here with us? How do we know we can trust him?"

"I don't know," Bill replied. The timing couldn't have been worse. "Maybe let's just wait and see who we get first."

Late that night, Bill woke to the sound of boots crossing the muddy ground outside their hut. The door slammed open and Bill counted three pairs of boots thudding across the uneven floorboards. Two were undoubtedly guards, but the third man's gait was ponderous, stumbling.

The guards left, leaving the stranger alone with them.

Owen wouldn't have heard them enter, but the freezing wind that came through the door was enough to rouse him. Bill heard his feet touch the floorboards.

"Jesus," Ade swore. "Reilly fucking *Burns*?"

Bill climbed out of his bunk, his heart beating wildly. "Are you serious? Reilly, is that you?"

The man gave no answer.

"I think he might be deaf," said Ade.

Bill found his way over to their new hut-mate and grasped him by the forearm. "I can't hear anything," said Reilly, his words thick and slurred.

"Over here," said Bill, guiding him to the table and helping him sit. Ade's crutches clicked as he came over to join them, half-falling into another chair.

Owen came to stand beside Bill, rapidly pressing letters into his skin. *It's Reilly Burns.*

Bill touched Owen's face and turned towards him. "I know. He's deaf. Go get your slate – we need to find out what's happened to him."

Bill tried to steady his thoughts while Owen hurried back to his bunk. A lot of people had looked up to Burns, until he disappeared during the first wave of arrests.

Owen returned with the small slate board he used to communicate with people from outside their hut. Bill heard the scrawl of chalk as Owen wrote out a question.

"They caught up with me a couple of weeks ago," Reilly said. His tone was ponderous and careful, presumably because he couldn't hear his own voice. "I was in a safe house, in Birmingham, helping to organise a strike. Unity troops stormed the place but I was the only one they caught. I refused to give them any names, so they took my hearing away."

Owen pressed fingers into Bill's arm. *We can take him with us. We can trust Reilly.*

"Of course," said Bill. This was Reilly Burns, after all, famous – or infamous, depending on your politics – for his stirring denunciation of National Unity in Parliament, just days before they seized power. If they could trust anyone, thought Bill, they could surely trust him. And yet he felt a powerful sense of disquiet, although he could not have said why.

Burns had his own questions, of course. He learned Bill's blindness was a punishment for articles he'd written denouncing National Unity. Ade had refused to disclose the names of fellow musicians who'd similarly spoken out. Owen, by contrast, was a computer technician who'd never learned the reason for his arrest.

"How long have you all been here on this island?" asked Burns.

"Nearly two years," said Ade. He spoke for Bill's benefit, chalking the words down for Reilly and Owen to read. "We're stuck here unless we give them names we don't even have."

"What about the rest of the inmates?"

Bill shook his head. "Most are regular prisoners – people caught hoarding or scavenging. There are mines on the Greenland coast that opened up when the ice melted. Most of them wind up there after a couple of months."

Ade paused in his writing. "We should tell Reilly," he said to Bill. "About our escape plan."

"I'm not sure."

"Why not?" Ade insisted. "Reilly Burns is a goddamn hero! Nobody else had the balls to say the things he did, even when he knew what would happen to him."

"Let me talk to my contact first," Bill insisted.

"What are you saying?" slurred Reilly, watching them argue.

"Tell him we're trying to figure out why they brought him here," said Bill, suddenly realising what had so disquieted him. Reilly's skin smelled of soap – the same one Hannegan used.

Not that that meant anything on its own, of course. But it was perfumed, and utterly unlike the coarse stuff they gave them in the camp.

"Ask him," said Bill, "if he spoke with Hannegan."

Scritch scratch. "No," said Reilly, after a short pause.

"Not at all? A woman with red hair and very pale skin?"

"No," Reilly repeated. "I don't know that name."

Reilly Burns was lying. Bill felt it deep in his bones. They'd taken his sight, but he'd gained so much more; the helmet had made him into a human lie detector. The same enhanced senses had warned him when O'Hare was about to lash out at Ade. He could smell the deceit on Reilly's breath, commingled with the perfumed scent of the soap.

Even then, Bill wanted to believe he was wrong. A part of him wondered if perhaps his senses weren't as accurate as he had come to believe; perhaps there was some other, perfectly reasonable explanation.

If only he could think of one.

Owen gave Reilly his bunk for the night, taking a thin blanket for himself and curling up on the hard floorboards. Reilly slept like the dead, which made it easier for Bill to slip out before dawn, carefully prying up first one loose floorboard, then another, pausing from time to time when Reilly shifted or muttered in his sleep. He could sense Ade watching him silently in the dark from his own bunk.

Bill climbed down into the narrow space beneath the hut, which stood on pilings. A gorse bush had grown up next to their hut, obscuring a section of the barbed-wire fence that surrounded the camp. Some weeks before, Bill had sneaked down on several successive nights and had dug a shallow pit under the fence where the bush hid it from view. There was just enough of a gap that he could squirm his way under the wire.

He emerged outside the camp and scuttled through wild grass, bent low. His blindsight told him it was a moonless night, and he tasted salt from the Atlantic. The freezing wind blowing across the island, somewhere off the coast of Scotland, was enough to shrivel the skin beneath his shirt.

The remains of a village stood just a few hundred metres from the camp. He made his way to a house just above the high tide-line; much of the village had become submerged over the years as the waters rose.

After its original occupants fled, the village had briefly served as an evacuation point for refugees escaping the plagues. Many of them had left their luggage behind, and a few months before, a number of the inmates had been set to digging through the half-rotted suitcases, keeping anything useful and heaping the rest in a pile to be burned.

Owen had found a child's toy computer, and risked serious punishment smuggling it back to their hut. It was a cheap little plastic thing, but it could be hand-cranked, and had some limited voice interactivity. To their shock, it worked on the first try. Owen, who had been a sysop before his arrest, even found a way to log undetected into the camp's network and send encrypted messages to the resistance on the mainland.

The computer was wrapped in oilskins, pushed to the back of a shelf in the sodden basement of the house. Keeping the computer anywhere inside the camp perimeter was out of the question: there was too much risk of it being found during a raid. And blind or not, in many ways Bill was the least handicapped of the three of them. He brought it up to the living-room and, crouched on the edge of a half-rotted table, cranked the machine's tiny pink plastic handle until it emitted a tinny bell-like sound.

Owen had set the machine up so that it spoke each letter when he pressed it. He'd had enough practice by now it didn't take too long to compose an email and send it.

Reilly Burns arrived at camp, he wrote. *Took us by surprise. Should we bring him?*

The reply came only minutes later. Sometimes he waited hours.

Bring him to evac point if it's safe. We'll make room. Is he in good health?

They took away his hearing. Can I give him any news? He thought for a moment. *Does he have any family? Anyone on the outside he needs to know about?*

Another long wait followed. He blew on his hands, then tucked them into his armpits. Surprise raids on the huts were not unknown, although there hadn't been one in months. If one was ordered tonight, it would be worth all their lives if they discovered him missing.

The reply finally came. *No such news. His family all died in a Unity camp on the Isle of Man two years ago.* The computer read the words out in a childish falsetto.

Bill shut the computer down, put it back in its oilskins, then sat back on his haunches, thinking. Planning their escape had taken months. Just twenty-four hours from now, they'd slip under the fence and board a trawler that would carry them to Europe.

Bill made his way back to camp, taking care not to make a sound as he climbed back through the floorboards. He needn't have worried: Reilly was still sleeping the sleep of the dead.

Reilly accompanied them to the canteen later that morning. Bill held onto his sleeve, so Reilly could "guide" him there. Bill didn't need the help, of course, but he didn't want Reilly, or anyone else, to know that.

"Is it safe to talk here?" asked Reilly once they were all gathered around a table.

"It's noisy," Bill said quietly, sipping his broth. "That helps." He heard Ade scratching the words onto Owen's slate before showing them to Reilly.

"Is our hut bugged?"

Bill shrugged. "I don't think anyone cares enough about us out here at the end of the world. Mostly, we get left the hell alone – although I think Hannegan is looking to change all that."

"Who is she?" asked Reilly, reading Owen's slate.

Bill could taste the man's evasiveness.

"She strikes me as the kind of person," said Bill, "who thinks she can get results where others can't."

"These people…" Reilly made an exasperated sound. "That thing they call the helmet started out as a medical miracle, you know that?" Bill nodded. "A way to cure blindness, deafness, a list of ailments and disabilities a mile long."

"And they turned it into a weapon," muttered Ade. "That's Unity for you."

"You had a family, right?" Bill asked, not caring if the question seemed abrupt. "What happened to them?"

"I…" Reilly's sudden indecision tasted tart and sharp, like he couldn't figure out the right response. "They were arrested and put in a camp. They… they died."

"Jesus," said Ade. "I'm sorry."

"I'm sorry too," said Bill, fighting not to show his confusion and anger. Reilly was lying – which probably meant his family were still alive, whatever the resistance seemed to think.

Bill had never had a family of his own, and had no idea what he might be capable of in order to keep them safe. Perhaps he should have felt sorry for Reilly Burns. Perhaps.

Bill and Ade leaned on each other as they walked back to the hut, the others following a few steps behind. "Don't tell Reilly about the escape," Bill muttered.

Ade became suddenly tense. "Why?"

"He said his family are dead. They aren't."

"How do you…?"

"Believe me when I say he's lying. Unity must have kept them alive, and now they're using them to control Reilly. We've all heard stories of them doing the same thing to other people. We have to assume he's a spy."

"How can you be so damn *sure*?"

"The same way I always am."

Later that evening, the first raid in months was carried out while the inmates were all getting their evening rations. When Bill and the others got back to their hut, they found their bunks pushed aside, their mattresses lying outside on the damp gravel.

Bill got down on his hands and knees and pressed his fingers against the floorboards that gave him access to the outside world. There was no sign they had been pulled up, no scent belonging to any of the guards. He closed his eyes in silent relief.

If Reilly had wondered what he was doing, pressing and sniffing at the floorboards, he didn't ask. "It's Hannegan," said Bill, standing back up. "Everything's been different since she arrived."

If only he could figure out what it was she wanted.

Not long after they'd pushed the bunks back into place and dragged the mattresses back in, two guards came to escort Bill back to the main building. Inside, he scented several other inmates all waiting to be questioned. He was led past all of them and straight into Hannegan's office.

"Mister Sharpe," she said. "We searched your hut."

He sat across from her, trying not to show how worried he was. "And?"

"We found nothing. But you interest me. The way you move around this camp, I could swear it's like you can see."

Bill chuckled to hide his nervousness. "Maybe you missed it, but your helmet made me blind. I can't see a damn thing."

"And yet we've had one or two reports of Senseless in other camps having their remaining senses extraordinarily heightened following their treatment. You can understand why that might be of great scientific interest."

"I don't see what it has to do with me."

"I've interviewed half a dozen inmates who witnessed your assault on Mister O'Hare. It's not the first time you've been seen acting precisely as if you were still sighted. As if you know exactly what's going on around you regardless."

As she spoke, Bill heard a drawer slide open, slowly, as if Hannegan was working hard to keep it as quiet as possible. He heard her feet move around the desk until she stood to one side of him.

Immediately he knew there was a gun to his head. He could picture its barrel hovering just an inch from his right ear.

"I have something in my hand, Mister Sharpe," said Hannegan. There was a slight edge of strain in her voice, no doubt, he thought, from holding the heavy weapon level with his skull. "Can you tell me what it is?"

Bill willed himself not to move, but thinking was far easier than doing. He couldn't ignore the thrill of alarm surging up his spine, or the shortness of his breath.

"I don't know," he said, his voice tight.

"I don't believe you."

He knew, just a moment before she did it, that she was going to shoot him. Instinct took over: he jerked away just as she squeezed the trigger, tumbling off his chair and onto the floor.

The breath rattled out of his throat in quick spasms. The gun had made a clicking sound and nothing more. "You tricked me."

"You've been tricking the idiots running this camp for a lot longer," said Hannegan. Her voice was colder now. "Go back to your hut and stay there until tomorrow morning."

And then? he nearly asked, but he already knew the answer. Then they'd put him in the one small motorboat the camp authorities kept fuelled by the dockside and send him back to the mainland, to have his brain picked apart.

But he'd be long gone by then – and not a moment too soon.

They let him out on his own, without even a guard to guide him back to his hut. It felt like Hannegan was laughing at him.

"Jesus," said Ade when he walked back in, "what the hell happened? You're shaking like a leaf."

"I need to talk to you," said Bill, ignoring Owen and Reilly. "Alone."

He led Ade back out into the chill evening air. He could easily imagine Reilly's puzzled stare as they closed the door behind them.

"She's onto me," said Bill. "She pulled a gun on me without any warning or sound and I flinched away from it before she pulled the trigger. It wasn't even loaded."

"*Jesus…*"

"I have an idea. We've got no choice but to take Reilly with us. If we don't and he realises we're gone, he might alert Hannegan before we can get to that trawler. But we won't tell him what we're doing until the moment we do it. If he tries to betray us or stop us, we'll… do whatever we have to. But if I'm somehow wrong about him, we can still all get away."

Ade swallowed hard. "So the plan's otherwise the same?"

Bill nodded. "A launch will be waiting to take us to the trawler from the beach on the far side of the village, but it's too risky for them to hang around more than a minute or two. If we're not there at the exact scheduled time, they'll leave without us."

"I just can't believe Reilly would inform on us," said Ade. "It goes against everything I know about him."

"Goddamn it, he lied to us about his family!" Bill hissed. "I smelled the same damn soap on his skin that Hannegan uses. The son of a bitch has been getting preferential treatment. Do you understand? It's him or us."

He heard Ade swallow. "Sure. I understand."

Bill didn't sleep that night. From the sound of their breathing, neither did any of the others – all except Reilly, who still had Owen's bed. When the time came, Bill rolled out of his bunk and pushed Owen awake. He grumbled and sat up.

Bill held up five fingers. "Five minutes," he mouthed, then did the same for Ade.

"What's going on?" asked Reilly, when Bill pushed him awake.

Bill pressed a hand over Reilly's mouth, then put a finger to his lips.

"What's happening?" Reilly demanded, too loudly. "What are you doing?"

Bill shook his head, then ignored him, waiting while Owen laced up his boots before doing the same for Ade. Then he helped Bill lever up the two long floorboards.

"You're *escaping?*" asked Reilly.

"I'll go first," Bill said, tapping his own chest, then pointing to the gap in the floor for Reilly's benefit. "Then you," he pointed at Reilly, and then at Owen and Ade, "then the others."

Bill slid down through the narrow gap before Reilly could say anything more. His knees pressed into damp soil and he squirmed beneath the floorboards towards the gorse bush. A body pushed through the gap behind him, and he heard Reilly cursing and muttering as he flailed around in the dark.

Bill crawled under the gap in the fence. Reilly came next, standing up and staring around. Ade followed, half-dragged by Owen.

Bill took Ade's other arm. It was always going to be slow going; Owen and Reilly at least could walk, but they'd have to carry Ade most of the way.

"This way," said Bill, pointing in the direction of the village.

Reilly grabbed Bill's free arm. "Why didn't you tell me?"

Bill shook him free, then tapped at his arm as if he were wearing a watch and mouthed the words *no time* at him.

"Of course there was time!" Reilly's speech was becoming more slurred; he'd been relying on the memory of what his voice sounded like in order to speak, and that memory was fading. "You didn't trust me."

Bill shook his head. There was nothing more he could say.

They reached the village. Bill felt the water lapping around his feet as they navigated a street. He could sense Reilly's amazement at the way he moved as easily as a sighted person.

Then they turned a corner, and then another, and Bill suddenly realised Reilly had slipped away. He heard the man's retreating footsteps as he hurried back in the direction of the camp.

"Reilly," said Ade, his voice urgent. "He's-"

"I know." The words felt heavy in Bill's mouth. He sniffed the air, cold and sharp in his nostrils. "Keep going," he told Ade. "Make sure you and Owen get to the rendezvous."

"But what about you?"

"Just get there," he snapped. "If he alerts the camp authorities, it won't just be our skins – it'll be everyone on that trawler as well."

Had he known this moment would come, he wondered? Could things have gone a better way, a way that didn't end in betrayal and death?

He didn't, couldn't, know. There was only this moment, and the next.

He pulled Ade into a tight embrace, then gave Owen a final nod before turning and hurrying back in the direction of the camp. It didn't take long for him to pick up Reilly's scent.

It soon became evident that Reilly had got lost in the dark. Bill could hear his laboured breathing, and followed the sound of his splashing feet down a side-street.

Bill stepped towards him and sensed Reilly's alarm. "I'm sorry," said Reilly. "I got lost. I–"

"You were trying to make your way back to the camp, weren't you?"

Reilly clearly didn't need his hearing to guess what Bill was saying. "You're not even blind, are you?" Reilly demanded, backing away.

"No, I *was* blind." Bill moved closer. "To certain realities, at least. Hannegan wanted you to spy on us, didn't she? That's why she put you in our hut."

Reilly couldn't hear him. It didn't matter. Without even thinking about it, Bill had bent down and scooped up a rock that felt heavy in his hand.

"You don't understand," said Reilly, his voice thick. "My family – they said they would…" He paused and let out a shuddering breath.

"I do understand." He heard the distant rumble of a motorboat engine as it approached the shore. "And I'm sorry."

Bill could almost taste the adrenaline spiking in the other man's bloodstream. Building up his courage.

Reilly came towards him then with a roar, splashing through the water. Bill anticipated him easily in the moonless dark, dodging out of his way. Reilly stumbled and fell hard as Bill kicked him from behind.

"I'm truly sorry," said Bill, then brought the rock crashing down on Reilly's head, again and again.

A little while later, he made his way to the rendezvous and listened to the sound of a motorboat engine growing faint with distance. He sat down with his back to a wall and stared out towards the ocean, letting the rain wash the blood from his face.

Just before dawn came the wail of a siren, and the sound of voices from the camp, coming closer.

Since becoming a professional science fiction writer in 2004, **Gary Gibson** has produced ten novels, including *Final Days*, *Extinction Game, and Stealing Light*. His forthcoming novel, *Survival Game*, a sequel to *Extinction Game*, was published by Tor in August 2016. He is a Glaswegian by birth and also by inclination.

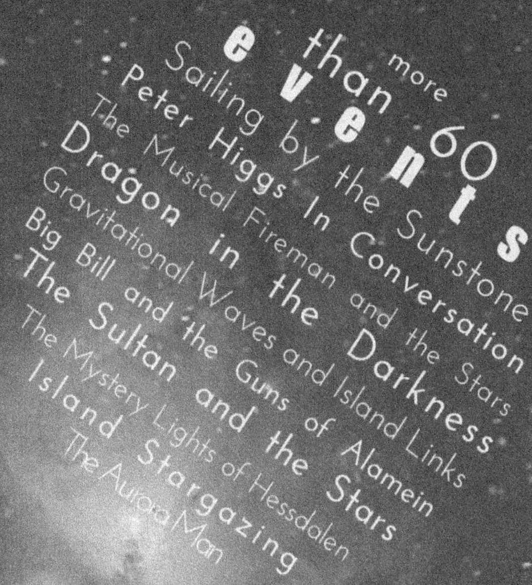
A world of enjoyment in
ORKNEY International SCIENCE FESTIVAL
7 - 13
SEP
2017
more than 60 events
Sailing by the Sunstone
Peter Higgs In Conversation
The Musical Fireman and the Stars
Dragon in the Darkness
Gravitational Waves and Island Links
Big Bill and the Guns of Alamein
The Sultan and the Stars
The Mystery Lights of Hessdalen
Island Stargazing
The Aurora Man
More Information on
www.oisf.org
www.frontiersmagazine.org

New Gray Ring to Join Olympic Five

Ada Palmer

Lausanne, Switzerland, June 12th 2275

The International Olympic Committee revealed today that a gray ring will be added to the iconic Olympic rings, in honor of the upcoming 2280 Winter Games to be held in Esperanza City, Antarctica.

Designed in 1912 by Olympic co-founder Pierre de Coubertin, the five traditional rings represented the five inhabited continents. The IOC announced plans for a new flag three years ago when they announced the victory of the Esperanza City bid. The campaign for the Olympic flag to add a sixth ring for Antarctica first gained international attention in 2226 when handball player Maxi Aviator Diáz became the first Antarctic-born athlete to win Olympic gold, and wore the medal with the Olympic Rings obscured by a sticker bearing the Antarctic flag.

The flag's six original colors – blue, yellow, black, green, and red with a white background – were intended to include the colors of every nation in the world. This was largely true in 1912, when flag designs dated to the pre-industrial period, when the need for long-distance visibility at sea favored bold, distinct colors, and when natural dyes struggled to consistently produce mixed tints such as orange or purple, or distinct shades such as navy blue and cyan blue. Speculation about the new color had focused on purple, orange, or cyan or sky blue, a popular color in modern flags, symbolizing the sky, global cooperation and internationalism, in contrast with dark or navy blues associated with oceanic empires, and with the tradition of revolution stemming from the French tricolor.

On the selection of gray, Olympic spokesperson Amur Yuu stated, "In addition to representing neutrality and universality in this age of internationalism and international law, the committee feels that gray represents the role of the Olympic Games as a public arena where human ambition is directed toward achievement instead of hostility, and where global tensions and controversies are aired and explored without violence or disrespect. If white symbolizes the ideal of peace, gray may symbolize conflict advanced positively and constructively, without war." When asked whether gray also represented the ice of Antarctica, Yuu stated that no ring is supposed to represent a specific continent, and that the committee hopes that people will associate the new ring, not with Antarctica, but with the shared human achievement of bringing safe and sustainable habitability to another portion of the globe.

Yuu firmly denied that gray is meant to represent the Moon. This question reflects allegations, which have haunted the Esperanza City bid, that members of the committee received substantial financial kickbacks from several lunar and extraterrestrial construction companies. Extraterrestrial construction groups have received more than 75% of the contracts for the construction of the new Olympic village and event venues, and bank statements leaked in March of last year confirm that the Esperanza City Committee has received more than €350,000 from the Luna City Tourism Board alone. The Esperanza City Olympic facilities will make unprecedented use of extraterrestrial technologies, and designs for the Olympic village show that a prominent space has been set aside to let these extraterrestrial contractors advertise their services and technologies. In response to allegations of corruption, spokesperson Ónix Silva Tapia stated, "Safety technology tries to be invisible, but we think visitors should see and understand how much went into making these games possible and safe. These first Antarctic games are not only about the athletes, but about the scientists, innovators, laborers, and explorers – on Earth and in space – whose efforts made this possible."

When asked about the possible lunar associations of the gray ring, astronaut Kuiper Freeport answered, "In that case it should be orangey brown – Mars is the real source of most of the innovations that have made life in Antarctica practical, not the Moon. If you want to learn to live a freezer you do it in another freezer, not a vacuum chamber."

The new six-ringed flag will be unfurled for the first time at the end of next year's Winter Games in Durban South Africa, whose committee has also been rocked by allegations of corruption surrounding the financing of refrigeration equipment. Durban will host a retirement parade for the five-ringed flag, featuring historic flags including the original Antwerp Flag flown in 1920. The parade will also feature 170 teachers from schools that have used old Olympic facilities from the 170 Summer or Winter Olympic Games at which the five-ringed flag has flown during its 350 year history. Spokesperson Yuu confirmed that the historic five-ringed flag will continue to fly at historic host cities, at portions of future opening and closing ceremonies, and at Olympic museums.

Ada Palmer is an author of science fiction and fantasy, a historian, and a composer. Her first science fiction series "Terra Ignota" (published by Tor Books) mixes Enlightenment-era philosophy with traditional science fiction speculation to bring to life the year 2454, not a perfect future, but a utopian one, threatened by cultural upheaval. The first volume, Too Like the Lightning, is nominated for science fiction's highest accolade, the Hugo Award, and Ada has also been nominated for the John W. Campbell Award for Best New Writer. She studies the long-term evolution of ideas and the history of religious radicalism, science, and freethought, especially in the Italian Renaissance, Enlightenment, and Classical Greece and Rome. She teaches in the History Department at the University of Chicago, and did her Ph.D. at Harvard University.
Ada composes close harmony folk music with mythological, science fiction and fantasy themes, and performs with the a cappella group Sassafrass. She also studies the history of manga anime, especially the "God of Manga" Osamu Tezuka, blogs for Tor.com and writes the history/philosophy blog ExUrbe.com.

First published in Shoreline of Infinity 5

Incoming

Thomas Clark

Art: Dave Alexander

Andy had just got off to sleep when it started again. It was getting to be every night now. He staggered out of bed, pulled his wax jacket on over his pyjamas. It could only have been three o'clock. Blearily, he stared at the Daedalian knots of his laces, tucked them down into the sides of his shoes. The close lights were broken, but the stairwell was already bright with open doors.

"Mornin, Mrs. McGraw," he shouted at the first door. Mrs. McGraw glowered at him, her weathered fist clasping shut her nightie like a brooch.

"Ah'll gie ye morning! It's a bloody disgrace, so it is," she said, "There's ma man daein mornins and he cannae get a wink o sleep."

"Ah ken, ah ken," Andy said, "Ah'm just away doon tae see aboot it."

"Aye, well, when ye see him ye can tell him fae me..."

The noise, a continual low hum which shook the windows in their settings, suddenly redoubled, driving out all competing sounds. As he passed down through the stairwell, Andy tried not to notice the faces that stared lividly at him from the cracks of doors, the horrific writhings of their silent mouths. By now the noise was so loud that his eyes quivered in their sockets, and the close had the freakish appearance of double exposed film, an art-house installation for the criminally insane. "Sorry, sorry, sorry," he found himself whispering as he shuffled past the doors, each framing a scene of suspended domesticity warped into something grotesque.

Outside, on the street, it was just as bad. Fractals of window-light pocked the low clear night, and the noise boomed through the narrow roads as they sunk towards the fields. As he walked along, Andy took a glance at the town hall spire. The clock was usually wrong, but it was certainly well past four. On the farms beyond Hawick, hired hands were already rising: Bulgarians and Poles who washed their faces in freezing water and listened with wonder to the sound, which could be heard as far as Branxholme Castle. It wasn't until the valleys towards Galashiels that the noise finally passed beyond the range of human hearing, although the Jedburgh dogs still whined, and the sheep in Selkirk bleated sympathy. No-one knew.

"It's not on, Andy, ah'm tellin ye," Johnny McEwan roared out of his window, "Ah'm on the phone tae the cooncil first thing. As if it's no bad enough UHRRRR"

Johnny threw his hands to his ears, but Andy knew from experience that nothing short of industrial grade ear muffs could block out this new noise: a long metallic shriek like a thousand rusty brakes. As the old man fell to his knees groaning, Andy pointed at an imaginary watch.

"Ah ken, Mr. McEwan, ah ken," he shouted, "Ah'm just away tae tell him. It's past a joke, this."

By the time Andy had turned the corner onto the high street, the noise had stopped, lingering only in the high arches of the town walls, like a trapped bird trying to get out. D-CON, who had never shown the slightest bit of interest in it before, was crouched down next to the 1514 Memorial, scanning its inscription raptly. Darkness once again had settled.

"Like butter widnae melt, eh," Andy said, "Whit's the game here then, pal? Whit's wae aw the noise?"

D-CON looked down at Andy with an immoderate start, as if only just noticing him.

"WHY ANDREW, I WAS…"

"Shh! Shh!" Andy whispered, the concrete shifting tectonically beneath his feet. The robot started again.

"APOLOGIES, ANDREW. WHAT NOISE?"

Andy screwed up his face.

"What noise? You got selective super-hearing all of a sudden? You're at it, big man. Ah've telt ye wance, ah've telt a hunner times – when it gets dark, folk are tryin to sleep."

"ANDREW, I CANNOT SLEEP."

"Name o God… Whit, you want me to sing you a lullaby?"

"I…"

"Ah'm jokin," Andy said hastily, "Ah ken whit you mean. But look, if you're no able tae sleep at night, can you no just dae whit everybody else does an watch the telly or somethin? Get any channel ye like wae aw that gear stickin oot yer heid. Ah mean… och, here we go."

A Volvo driving the wrong direction up the one-way street came to a sudden halt across the road. After a moment's struggle, a fat man with unkempt hair and a provost's chain over his nightgown wrangled his way out from under the steering-wheel and waddled over towards them. The backs of his slippers made a soft padding noise on the tarmac.

"Right, Andy! Whit's going on here? Giein ye any problems, is he?"

"Naw, Davie, it's just…"

"This is no good enough, Andy. It's needing nipped in the bud, like. Bloody robot getting the run of the place. Honest tae God."

Davie squinted in D-CON's direction. There were marks on either side of his nose where his glasses normally sat. He shook his head.

"Nae wunner his name's C-CON. C-CON, is it! It's enough tae seeken onybody. Ah'm telling ye, Andy…"

"His name's D-CON," Andy said, "Like Deacon Blue."

"Ah'm tellin ye, Andy," Davie continued, "Folk've just aboot had enough o this. D'ye have any idea how much it's costing us tae keep him?"

"Well, he's solar-powered, Davie, so…"

"Solar power!" Davie spat, "In Hawick? That's a joke! He's suckin this toon dry. An as for…"

"IF I FLEW INTO THE SUN," the robot interrupted, "I COULD RECHARGE TO FULL CAPACITY WITHOUT…"

"Aye, that'll be shining bright!" Davie veered slowly round, lifting up his eyes rather than his head. "Efter aw the money we've spent, we're just gonnae let ye fly away! D'ye think ma heid buttons up the back or sowt? Fly away, he says!"

Davie shook his head again, as if it was the only point of articulation his body had. His arms were folded so high across his chest that his chin was almost resting on them, and he was breathing heavily. Andy cleared his throat.

"Look, Davie," he said, "We cannae have it both ways. If we want tae keep him to ourselves, that's fair enough, but somebody's got to foot the bill. That's just economics."

"Oh aye?" Davie said without looking at him, "Get that aff your da, did ye? Dead smart, your da. Dunno how he's only working in a chippy."

With one last glower at D-CON, Davie turned on his heel and walked back across the road. Andy, whose cheeks had become a lipstick pink, looked up at the robot and smiled awkwardly. He always forgot that D-CON did not have emotive facial expressions or, for that matter, emotions.

The provost's car coughed and spluttered back into life. Like the provost himself, it had been serving in its official capacity for as long as Andy could remember. With much uncomfortable to-ing and fro-ing, Davie squeezed an arm between his bulk and the door and jerkily rolled down the window.

"Oh, aye, and while ah remember," he said, "Where are we at wae they comet things?"

The robot stared up into the sky.

"REPORT. NEAR-EARTH OBJECTS OBSERVED. QUANTITY: THREE. VELOCITY: 110 KILOMETRES PER SECOND. TIME OF IMPACT: 4.2 DAYS. CURRENT VISIBILITY FROM EARTH: ZERO. EXPECTED SURVIVAL RATE WITHIN IMPACT ZONE: ZERO. EXPECTED IMPACT ZONE: GALASHIELS."

Davie nodded in satisfaction.

"Right, that's a Wednesday then, eh? Ah'll let the bus drivers ken."

"Davie, d'ye no think…"

"Not a chance! Forget it!" Davie said, "Where were they when *we* were the wans aboot tae get smashed intae bits? Couldnae look the other way quick enough then! For aw they kent oor goose was cooked, an they never even lifted a finger. *They* didnae ken it wisnae a comet." He stared at D-CON bitterly, and shook his head. "Ah'll tell ye whit, though, ah wish it had've been."

After a few growls, the provost's car lurched off into the beginnings of the morning. Wisps of red had started to gather round the edges of the rooftops, and the unfathomable dark of the sky was about to break. As D-CON stood there, still gazing into the remnants of the night, Andy stared up at him.

"A hunner an ten kilometres a second? That's gey fast even for a comet, is it no?"

"IT IS."

Andy puffed his cheeks out thoughtfully.

"Jeez oh. Ah could see the point if it wis heading the ither wey. Ah've broke the sound barrier masel gittin oot o Galashiels." He smiled for a moment at the robot's unreflecting face, then let it drop. "Ach, no that Hawick's much better. But it's hame, eh? Ye ken everybody."

He paused as if conscious of having said the wrong thing, but D-CON showed no sign of having noticed. Andy let his hand rest on the monument's pedestal, tracing its inscription. It was too dark to read, and written in Latin, but he knew it off by heart. *From out of the depths it emerges, beautiful.*

"Do… do ye never get hamesick yersel, sometimes?"

"NO. ALL THINGS MUST FIND A PURPOSE, AND I HAVE FOUND MINE ON EARTH. I SHALL BE AT HOME HERE, BEFORE LONG."

Andy instinctively patted the robot on its leg, somewhere about its knee. The metal was light and soft to the touch, like aluminium, and strangely warm.

"Ah went tae New York, wance," he said, "Thought aboot Hawick the hale time. Couple o hours on a plane an it felt like the ends o the earth. Ach, but the sights, man! Ken the Statue of Liberty?"

D-CON lifted up its arm, and its hand was blue with light.

"FROM HER BEACON-HAND GLOWS WORLD-WIDE WELCOME…"

Andy smiled up into the lantern. Its beam was bright enough to shine the stars, but no-one else had chosen to see it. He shook his head.

"Never you mind, pal. You're daein alright. It's them buggers just need tae get used tae ye. But they'll get there, D-CON."

"B-CON."

"Eh?"

"MY NAME IS B-CON."

As Andy followed the robot's stare into the now starlit sky, a bat, suddenly visible against the gleam, fluttered past, and the air took on the pungent taste of lead. Never before had he witnessed skies so full of life, a horizon that brimmed with anything but streetlights and the cracks between curtains. Now, above the spire, three dots of light were developing slowly against the black, a perfect triangle that shimmered in the sky and hung there. He watched them coming, as if a fresh constellation was jostling into the order of things, a spearhead advancing through the aging cosmos.

He understood.

Beneath his palm, Andy felt the robot humming gently – happily, even. The stars were dying, and the news of some unfamiliar galaxy was finally reaching Earth.

Thomas Clark is a poet and writer from the Scottish Borders. His first poetry collection, *Intae the Snaw*, was published by Gatehouse Press in 2015. He is poet-in-residence at Selkirk Football Club and Scots co-editor at Bella Caledonia. He blogs at www.thomasjclark.co.uk

---

ALEXANDER '17

First published in Shoreline of Infinity 7

3.8 Missions

Katie Gray

Art: Dave Alexander

The wind screamed in and out the remains of buildings. It tugged at his clothes, whistled through the holes punched in his helmet for the strap, rattled his ear drums. There'd be a lull in the fighting, if he'd timed this right, but he could hear cracks of missiles in the distance. And there were mines, and sizzling pools left by chemical weapons, and the iSoldiers.

He skittered down a rubbly slope and checked his scope. The signal was a blip and fading. Lock on. Point two clicks, north-north-east. His scope fritzed and he shook it, cursing. The static cleared. He looked up.

The iSoldier was standing over him, a towering figure silhouetted against the burnt-orange smog. The flickering light from a nearby fire danced in its armour, black and gold. He couldn't tell if it was one of theirs. It was armed. Wrist gun. If he bolted it would shoot him dead.

Procedure. He rooted his feet to the ground and held up his wrist to show off his insignia. "Identify."

Like a panther, the iSoldier leapt from the wall. *Snap*. Its wrist-gun retracted. Reaching out, he touched its chestplate. "Identify."

A buzzing. "*Niner-niner-triple-three-delta.*"

"Right," he said, almost relaxing. "As you were."

Its hand shot out, grabbing his vest, knocking all the air out of his lungs. He cried out, gabbling nonsense like, "Friend!" and "On your side!" and "Reds, see? Reds!"

It tugged aside the strap of his vest to get a visual reading of his rank insignia. *Private Carter, Tracey. F-Tech.*

Thump. He dropped to the ground like a discarded sack. In a single leap, the iSoldier bounded over the wall.

"Wanker," Tracey said aloud. It didn't make him feel any better. He adjusted the straps of his vest and levered himself upright.

He checked his scope. Point two klicks. Signal still fuzzy.

He ducked between barbed wire and broken masonry into the chewed-up remains of what had been a car park. He crouched, scanning the open space.

There. A pair of metallic legs spilling out from behind the skeleton of a car. He picked his way over, staying low, and stared at what was left of the iSoldier he'd been sent to patch up.

The legs – just the legs, and a spray of still-hissing fluid. For a happy moment he thought that was all that was left, that the rest of the iSoldier was being ground to dust in the belly of a Beast.

But maybe ten metres further he saw the arms and torso, wires and nerve-enhancements spilling out like tentacles. It was like a broken toy, a rag doll torn in half and left in the dirt.

"Well," he said, "That's going to take some fixing."

Crouching to inspect the legs, he saw the tail end of the spinal cord, white bones visible within the dense circuitry. The only thing left to do was call salvage.

His scope clicked. *Signal online.* He spat a curse. Now he had to check its neural functioning.

The torso was motionless, ragged, but procedure was procedure. He crawled to it. "Identify."

No response. He put his hand on its chestplate.

"Identify, soldier."

Nothing. Sometimes skin contact helped, when the sensors weren't at optimum. He stripped off his glove, but jerked back. The armour was searing hot.

Groping at his belt, he unhooked his probe and forced the helmet open. The face beneath was pale and screwed up, the sound of its panting high and dull in the murky air.

"Identify! Hey!" He patted at the side of its skull. "Status report."

Its eyes opened. "What?" Its voice was an echo of itself, electronics and human vocal cords.

"Identify."

"I don't understand." The electronic voice was flat. The human voice was thick with pain.

Tracey should have realised, then, what had happened. "Identify yourself." Nothing. He detached his scope and held it over the iSoldier's eye, trying for a retinal scan. "Hold still."

976-555-λ.

Oh, no. Jesus, Mary, Joseph and all the Saints in heaven, no. He closed his eyes, swallowed, his throat clasping, dry. It didn't matter, it couldn't matter. The iSoldier didn't even remember.

"I can't feel my legs." Tracey looked down at it hazily, thinking the status report command had kicked in at last and wondering why it wasn't following procedure. "Why can't I feel my legs?"

One last time. "Identify."

"What?" The iSoldier made a noise like it was trying to clear its throat. It was confused by the crackly echo.

"Who are you? What's your name?"

"Private McCray. Eight-oh-oh-niner-fifty."

Tracy almost threw up. Right there, on top of the iSoldier. This couldn't be real. His brain was helpfully scrolling through all the reasons why this shouldn't be possible, all the safeguards in place to ensure iSoldiers never did this, ever.

"Why can't I," said the iSoldier, "What –" It shuddered, and screamed – half staticky roar of electronics, half animal pain.

Tracey covered his ears.

He'd scrapped iSoldiers before. He ought to call salvage, the iSoldier was a tattered mess of fractured spine and chewed-up neural circuits. All he had to do was make the call.

The ever-present rumbling was growing louder. As he dithered, the iSoldier's static-riddled cries were drowned out by the *screeeeech* of bladed wheels chewing through concrete.

"Oh, God!"

The Beast loomed, a misty, disjointed shadow in the fog. He could hear its jaws clashing.

"Oh, Jesus Christ."

Was it Red or Blue? It didn't matter. It didn't care, he didn't care. He was on his feet, ready to run like hell for base, when hot metal closed around his ankle. The iSoldier's hand. It couldn't have seen the Beast, but could hear it, feel it shaking the ground.

"Don't leave me here, you can't leave me here–"

"You're *scrap iron*!" He didn't know if the iSoldier heard him over the pulsing roar of oncoming blades but its brown eyes stared up at him, jerking back and forth in their sockets, alive.

It was the eyes that did it.

Tracey heaved the iSoldier across the tarmac, towards the wreck of the nearest building. It was dead weight, so hot he could feel the heat radiating through his gloves. It was screaming. He thought it was screaming at the Beast but it was screaming at itself. He'd lifted its shoulders and it was looking down at its body, looking at the mass of cables trailing from its severed abdomen, at the void where its legs had been, and its chest plate was vibrating with its screams.

The Beast was almost on them, churning a path through the city, flames and smoke belching out of its grilled mouth. It ate. It gorged itself on rubble and concrete and steel and toxic goo. Tightening his grip, Tracey staggered fast as he could for shelter.

The ground rocked, cracks opened up in the hellish force of its approach, and he fell.

He tumbled down a rubbly slope into the black emptiness that had once been the basement. Gravel and dust fell around him and he curled in on himself, covering his airways. The stink of the fumes, the agonising roar in his lungs, the heat, the dampness of the concrete, the *noise*. It was so loud it wasn't even sound, it was pure, vile sensation pounding at his eardrums, incessant.

When it quieted, he found with dull surprise that he was still alive. He took deep breaths, sobbing in relief, coughing up mouthfuls of dust. He opened his eyes. The Beast hadn't crushed the wall completely. Here and there shafts of sunlight branched through. He might be able to dig himself out.

He heard the iSoldier, still screaming at the top of its lungs. Tracey checked his scope. It was flickery, but functional. Two Red blips, Blues all around them. iSoldiers from the belly of the Beast. If they'd picked up Tracey's signal they'd have come for him already. Sooner or later they'd hear the noise.

He dragged himself over to the iSoldier, wincing as the concrete scraping his raw knees. "Shut up," he gritted out. "Shut up, shut up, *shut up*." He banged on its armour. "You need to be quiet! They'll hear you!"

"Oh, God," said the iSoldier. "Fuck, *fuck*, my legs, where are my *legs*?" It made choked gulping sounds, forcing air back into its failing lungs.

"Will you *shut up*?"

It said, "I can't," and, "Sorry," and, "Hurts." Tracey clawed at the back of its neck, holding his probe between his teeth as he tried to find the right spot to – *yes* – open it up, exposing the cluster of wires at the top of its spine. "What are you doing?"

The wires were half-fused, a tangled mess of still-cooling slag. There was only one thing to do.

"I'm sorry." He jammed in his probe, right up against the first joint of its spine. "This'll only hurt a lot." He thumbed the button.

It screamed, a jagged wail of electronics, arms flexing madly. Somewhere in the mass of trailing cables below its waist something sparked.

And it was done, and the iSoldier was gasping, harsh mechanical sobs falling from its lips. Heat pulsed off its shell. "Oh, God. What did you do to me?"

"I'm sorry," said Tracey lamely. "I needed you to be quiet."

"I can't – it doesn't hurt any more. What did you do?" It flexed its fingers. "I can't feel anything."

"I fried your nervous system," said Tracey. "Needed you to shut up. You were going to get us caught."

The iSoldier's eyes rolled to look at him. "You look familiar."

"One of those faces."

It blinked, sucking in air noisily.

Tracey looked up at the tattered shell of the building, hoping that it would die now and let him be.

"Where are my legs?"

It was such a silly question, w*here are my legs*, like he'd just forgotten where he'd put them, and Tracey nearly laughed. "I don't know. They were outside, but that Beast probably crushed them."

It digested that. "What happened to me?"

"I don't know. You were in bits when I arrived."

"No, before that."

Tracey shuffled his feet in the dust and grime that coated the floor. He swallowed. His throat was dry. "How much do you remember?"

It wheezed. "I don't know. I was in this – place, I don't know where – they told me I'd been picked out for an experimental treatment, and then I was in a waiting room or – I don't know. It's all in bits. What did they do to me?"

The soft tissues went first. You scooped them out like pumpkins on Hallowe'en. Then the bones. Keep the arm bones and the ribcage and the skull and the spine, but the hip bones and the thigh bones went on the scrap pile, and then – "Oh, God. My *legs*."

Tracey steeled himself. He avoided its eyes. They were the only part of it that looked alive. "If it makes you feel any better, they weren't your original legs."

"Was that supposed to be funny?"

"Not really."

"What happened to my real legs?"

"They weren't used for the procedure. Leg bones – aren't. They don't – I'm sorry."

It was looking at its hands. It mouthed *procedure*.

"This wasn't an experiment, was it? I saw – others. How many people did you –"

"I don't know!" said Tracey. "A lot. Thousands. More, maybe. I'm just a field tech, alright? I don't know. They don't tell us anything. They barely even train us."

"They told you more than they told me."

"Shut up," Tracey snapped. "I should have left you out there. I don't know why I bothered saving you."

The iSoldier's eyes blazed . "Oh, you bastard," he said, "You sick, selfish, *fuck* –"

"You are *dead*!"

It went quiet.

"In case you hadn't noticed – you're already dead. Your spine's severed and your entire programming's gotten wiped somehow which means you're undergoing critical neural failure, so I give it maybe two or three hours before your brain disintegrates completely, except you don't *have* two hours. You're overheating. You've got maybe half an hour before what's left of your internal organs cook." He took deep breaths. "So yeah. You're basically dead and I'm basically not and if I'd just *left* you there I might actually have gotten out of this."

Staggering, he sank down on the concrete.

"You could call for help."

"No point. They won't come. They might've if there was enough left of you to save, but there's not, so they won't. They won't come for me. I'm expendable."

The iSoldier wheezed. "You said they didn't train you."

"What?"

"You said they didn't train you. Didn't sound like it just now."

"I was a junior medtech. I got demoted. Happy now?"

There were regulations about executing non-combatants. But there were jobs that needed doing, jobs too dangerous to risk an AI. Field techs, on average, lasted 3.8 missions before their sticky end. It was tidy. It worked, on average.

This was Tracey's fifth mission.

"I woke up on a battlefield without any legs, so no, I'm not happy." A choking sound that was either a laugh or a sob. "What did you do to get demoted?"

"What's it to you? Nothing. I didn't do anything. Piss off." Tracey didn't want to look at it. He didn't want *it* looking at *him*, not with those dancing, living eyes.

"You must have done something."

"Well, I didn't. It wasn't something I did, it was something I was supposed to do that I didn't. So I didn't do anything."

It was quiet for such a long time that he thought it might have died. The urge to look at it grew overwhelming.

"I remember – a room. It was grey. There were people. Other soldiers. We didn't know what was going on, but something wasn't right, and then something, something –" Its eyes flickered to Tracey's face. "You were there."

"No I wasn't."

"Yeah you were," it said. "You were there, you said I was to come with you, and then you took me into – the other place, and then you –"

"Shut up!" Tracey snapped, even though it wasn't saying anything. "I didn't want to. They made me do it, they ordered me, and when you don't do what they say – it wasn't my fault." He buried his face in his arm. "I didn't know when I signed up. I swear I didn't know."

"You were holding me down. You bastard. You doped me. You *bastard.*"

"Stop it," said Tracey. "Please – just leave me alone. I saved your life, didn't I?"

"Fuck you." It made a ghastly, wretched sound.

It was staring at its hands, at the smooth metal joints, and it was crying, or trying to cry. "How much of me is left?"

"I don't know." He scrubbed at his face. "Nervous system. Some of your skeleton. Heart and lungs, some muscle tissue. Not much soft matter. It's an extensive procedure." Human nervous system, mechanical body. Who could ask for a better soldier?

"This wasn't an experiment, was it? You knew what you were doing. This is – we were supposed to be the good guys. Aren't we the good guys?"

"I don't know any more. I don't know if we developed this or if we sneaked the technology from them. I'm not sure anyone even remembers."

"How long has it been? Is this the same war?"

Tracey choked out a grim laugh. "Oh, yeah. It's the same war alright. It never ends. It's been three years since – almost four. I remember 'cause…"

" 'cause what?"

"Because you were the first one I worked on." He breathed in, out. "I remember you. You were blond. Your teeth were crooked. I liked you."

"*Did* you?"

"You were – charming." *Charming*, a strange word to be using on a battlefield, it felt all wrong in his mouth. "Bit flirty. I thought you were fit." He almost smiled – but the memory triggered a wave of nausea.

The blood coating his latex gloves, the low whine of the equipment, the wet sounds it made as –

"I remember," it said. "You were shy. I like shy."

"I wasn't shy, I was piss-terrified," Tracey said, staring at his knees. "I didn't realise how much it was going to suck. Till I spoke to you." The air tasted of metal and spilt fuel. He could hear the iSoldier sobbing, a rough, grating sound.

It said, "What's your name?"

"Tracey Carter."

"Tracey's a girl's name."

"Fuck you, I saved your life."

"Tracey," it breathed. "Do me a favour, yeah? Don't tell anyone I cried over this."

He snorted out a laugh. "I don't think I'm going to be telling anyone anything."

"You could call for help." The electronics in its voice were warping.

"I already told you, they won't come for me."

"They might. You should try."

"Why do you even care what happens to me?" said Tracey. "I did this to you. I thought you hated me. You *should* hate me."

"Don't want to die hating you," said the iSoldier. "Don't want to die hating anyone."

It was looking at him. Maybe there were tears in its eyes, or maybe that was the way the light was reflecting. "Private McCray. That was your name?"

"Joseph McCray."

"I outrank you." He rubbed his hands over his eyes, up through his sticky hair. "Alright. Fine." He gave his scope a shake and groped through the functions. "I'm pinging the base. Happy now?"

"Yeah, I guess," said Joseph McCray. His metal hand touched Tracey's knee, trying to comfort. Tracey didn't move, because he didn't know what else to do, and because he kind of wanted comforting, even if was from a broken iSoldier.

The light was dimming. He wasn't sure if night was falling or if it was the thickening smoke. His scope flickered and died for good. He drank half the water he had left and ate his compacted nutrient bars.

He tried to climb out, dragging himself up the slope. He put his weight on a loose clump of brick and skittered all the way down, scraping

open his hands and knees. He picked the grit out of his palms and began again.

"You won't make it."

"Oh yeah?" He scrabbled to find footing, staring up at the rays of musty light. Freedom was so close he could taste it.

"It's like – I grew up near this old quarry. There was one side that was too steep to climb. We always tried but we never made it, it was like walking on ice – and one time my mate tried it and he fell and broke – my mate, he –" His growling voice cut out. Tracey lost his tenuous footing, slithering down to the concrete. "My mate, his name was – he was my best mate since forever, I should know his name – why don't I remember his name?"

"I dunno." Tracey dusted off his hands. He gave his scope a shake. Still nothing. He steeled himself. "Your memory centres might be starting to break down."

"No." Joseph waved a metal hand at him. "No, you said that wouldn't happen. You said I'd be dead first."

"Said you'd be dead before your neural circuits went kaput. Never said you'd be dead before you started to – you know. Go."

"Go *where*?" Joseph clutched at the ground, trying to lever himself upright. His fingers gouged tracks through the concrete. "What's going to happen to me?"

"I don't know. I don't know! You've still got most of your brain. I don't know anything about brains. I'm a tech, not a neuroscientist." He climbed. Hand, foot. Hand, foot.

"If you get out –" Joseph's voice was tinged with panic. Perhaps it always had been. The electronic voice box was fading, the iSoldier's voice falling to an unintelligible hum. "If you get out, are you just going to leave me here?"

Hand, foot. Hand, foot.

"I don't want to die like this. Not alone. Don't leave me to die like this alone, *please*."

His hand met something jagged under the dirt. He dragged himself upwards even as blood smeared on the dust, fuelling his screaming muscles with mind-numbing desperation. He hadn't known he wanted to live this badly.

He fell, tumbling like Jack down the hill. Something jarred in his arm. He cradled it to his chest. "You said yourself. I'm not going to make it."

"Did I?" There was a clicking sound. Tracey almost didn't recognise it as a gulp. "I don't remember."

Tracey rubbed at his face, trying to scrub away the dirt. The palm of his hand stung. His arm throbbed. He wiped his oozing nose on his wrist. He could smell something over the dank, dusty stench of the basement. It smelled like meat cooking. "Do you smell that?"

"Smell what?" said Joseph. "Can't smell anything."

"Yeah." Tracey kept his hand over his nose. "Probably for the best."

"Why? What is it?"

"Nothing." He tested his arm. It bent, but when he reached out a shock of pain jolted up to his shoulder. "I think I'm stuck here."

"You could call for help."

"I already did." He worked his arm, hoping it would get better if he stretched it, but it hurt more and more the more he moved it.

"Right."

Joseph brought a hand up in front of his face, flexing each finger-joint in turn. "Is that my hand?"

"Yeah." Tracey flexed his own fingers. It hurt.

"What happened to me?" said Joseph. "Why am I a robot? I don't – I don't remember what happened to me."

Tracey could hear a hissing, crackling sound coming from somewhere within Joseph's armour. The last of his cooling system giving way. He pressed a hand to his mouth and tried not to retch.

If he could get out – which was unlikely, with a busted arm – maybe, just maybe, he'd get back to base before the Blues got him. And then what? He'd live to die another day, blown into chunks or fried by a nerve-shell.

Or he could die here, cold and alone in what was left of a basement with what was left of an iSoldier.

The sizzling was getting louder.

Joseph let out a yelp. "What?" He was panting, in-out-in-out, rough gasps of air. "What – why can't I –" He was staring at his hand – but he wasn't. His eyes were roaming about in their sockets, unfocused. His optic nerve had severed.

Staggering over, Tracey knelt beside him. "What's wrong?"

"I can't see," Private McCray choked. "Oh God, I can't see."

Tracey took a deep breath. He tried to sound calm. "It's alright, Private. You're fine."

"Why can't I see? I remember – fighting. There was a blast. What happened to my eyes?"

"You got hit," said Tracey. "You'll be okay. I promise. I'm a medtech."

Maybe Joseph believed him, maybe he didn't. "What was it? Nerve shell?"

"Yeah. One of those bastards."

"I can't feel my legs, are they –"

"You're going to be fine. Just need some fixing, that's all." His voice was getting rough. God, he was thirsty. "I called for help, remember? There'll be more medics here any minute now."

"Yeah." Dark fluid seeped out of the corner of Joseph's mouth. "Listen, do me a favour and don't tell Sergeant Reid I cracked up over this."

"Don't worry. I can keep a secret." Tracey clutched his injured arm to his chest. The air around them shimmered. "I'll tell him you were stoic and manly throughout."

Private McCray laughed. He choked. The crackling was getting louder. "What's that noise. Feels like – air bubbles inside my skin."

"It's nothing, don't worry about it." Tracey could feel the heat coming off the armour on his face.

"Sounds like – sounds like steak cooking. Steak cooking. My Dad used to make it on Sundays. Days. Every and chips. Always – well done." He rasped. "Smells good."

"Yeah, yeah I know." Tracey hoped he sounded soothing. "You just relax now, Private. Help's coming."

"Not supposed to relax too much. When you're concussed, you're supposed to stay awake. Awake." A rumbling was building on the edge of Tracey's hearing. "You have to count."

"Count?" The light was going away, as if the sun was setting – or a shadow was looming.

"Between the thunder. Ever been struck by lightning?"

And he was gone. A light went out behind his eyes. Nothing left but the hissing and popping of his innards gently cooking themselves. Tracey prodded at his face, trying to get his eyes to close. He could only get one shut. The other hung open, like he was winking. He used the last of the charge in his probe to force the helmet.

It was just half an iSoldier, leaking steam and fluids onto the filthy concrete.

Tracey backed away. He found his canteen. His fingers shook as he unhooked it from his belt and slowly drank.

He could hear a distant roaring. There was no sense conserving water. He finished it off, guzzling what little was left. It spilled tepid down the front of his vest.

A minute passed in the building haze, fingers slipping on the damp plastic of his canteen, watching motes of brick dust dancing in the last rays of light till they were blotted out for good.

The roar of the Beast was almost upon him. Clawed feet tearing through steel and concrete, churning up the city to feed itself. It had to be just outside, it was so loud, but the noise kept on building, building till it hurt, till the whole world narrowed down to just the *roar* and the hurt.

He screamed into it till his throat was raw. He couldn't hear himself screaming, couldn't hear a thing until it stopped.

It quieted so suddenly he staggered, almost fell. He opened his eyes, squinting in the sudden light, in the dust-cloud than enveloped him. It had cracked open the building. It loomed over him, bigger than anything he'd ever seen. The low thrumming of the engines was distorted, as if he was under water. He unclasped his hands from his ears and found smears of blood in his palms. He hadn't even noticed.

A figure, stark against the light. Another, and another. iSoldiers. On the march.

He heard faint underwater sounds of metal dragging on concrete. They were dragging away what was left of Private McCray to be recycled. Something like hope fluttered in his chest. Maybe they'd come for him after all.

The nearest iSoldier was staring at him through the dusty, warped gloom the world had become. "Identify." His throat was raw, he could barely get the word out. He swallowed, coughed, tried again. "Identify!"

It raised an arm. In its wrist, a blue glow.

The shot was pure, searing agony, every nerve-ending in his body screaming at once, until he was gone, blank, empty –

He came to with cold concrete at his back, and noted with dull surprise that he was still alive. For a split second there was elation, elation at somehow clinging to consciousness despite everything –

The second blast coursed through him like a bucket of cold water. There was pain. There was nothing, a wave of numbness. There was enough time to think, to register that his nervous system was giving out under the strain, the nerve-shell was shutting it down, leaving him numb, and he thought, he thought –

– A *snap* of power. A spasm. A breath.

Tracey opened his eyes and saw white light. He couldn't move. There were wires in him, tiny hooks all over his body, holding him in place. There were people pacing around him.

He was still alive. Or – not *still* alive. Rolling his eyes upwards, chest heaving, he saw the RESC unit still sparking. *Of course*, he thought.

"Help me."

The figures in the room kept moving, kept circling him, like sharks. They were wearing masks over their faces.

Silence.

"Who are you?" There was an insignia on the RESC unit, but though he rolled his eyes up and squinted, he couldn't make out the colour. It looked a sickly purple.

A high-pitched whine. He knew that sound.

"What – no."

Apparatus glided into view, a squat box with blades and serrated wheels and needles, its arms swinging over him, and he knew that apparatus, it was nauseatingly familiar.

"No," he said. "No, you – you don't want me – I'm a medtech, not a soldier." He gulped down air, the sound of the apparatus powering up filling his ears. "Look at me – you don't want me – no, no no no no –"

The glistening point of a needle angled towards him and in the moment before it stabbed down, he saw that the people around him weren't wearing masks. Those were their faces, metallic, expressionless visors, and when he twisted, trying to escape the needle, he saw another helmet, set aside for him.

A pinprick of pain as the needle went in and as the world swam around him, he had time to think *right, of course*. Because there was no sense in fighting this, no sense in worrying about Blues and Reds. They'd already lost. All of them.

Katie Gray is an author of science fiction, fantasy and science-fantasy living and working in Edinburgh. She has a masters degree in creative writing from the University of Edinburgh. Her work has appeared in Orbis and Freak Circus and she's currently putting the finishing touches on a fantasy novel.

"Gender identity and sexuality in Current Fantasy and Science Fiction" is the first Call for Papers of Academia Lunare, the non-fiction arm of Luna Press Publishing.

The papers explore how society, as reflected in real life, literature, movies, TV, games and cosplay, is currently dealing with gender identity and sexuality in speculative fiction, asking an important question: do we have a problem?

Featuring papers from **Juliet E McKenna, Kim Lakin-Smith, Cheryl Morgan, A J Dalton, Jyrki Korpua, Hazel Butler, Lorianne Reuser, Anna Milon, Rostislav Kůrka** and **Alina Hadîmbu.**

Release date 09/08/2017

Science Fiction, Fantasy & Dark Fantasy in Fiction and Academia.

Scottish Independent Press.

Est. 2015

This anthology is the product of the first 'Steampunk Hands around the World' project, created by eleven international authors. It encouraged writers to engage with each other and to express how Steampunk, though global, is born from the unique culture of its setting.

To keep the flavour and individuality of the authors' voices, and with an eye on accessibility, Luna Press Publishing has created this bilingual anthology, half in Spanish and half in English, so that you too can shake hands in friendship with these incredible writers.

Featuring stories from: **Josué Ramos** - Spain; **Fábio Fernandes** - Brazil; **Marcus R. Gilman** - Germany; **Aníbal J. Rosario Planas** - Puerto Rico; **Ray Dean** - Hawaii; **César Santivañez** - Peru; **Milton Davis** - Africa; **Suna Dasi** - Scotland/India; **Elaine Vilar Madruga** - Cuba; **Petra Slováková** - Czech Republic; **Paulo César Ramírez Villaseñor** - Mexico.

Release date: 04/08/2017

SF Caledonia

Monica Burns

Have you ever heard of David Lindsay, Robert Ellis Dudgeon or Andrew Blair? What about John Buchan, Lewis Grassic Gibbon or Sir Arthur Conan Doyle? What these Scottish authors have in common is that they all produced works of early science fiction. SF Caledonia, is a unique series in *Shoreline of Infinity* in which I unearth these old and largely forgotten science fiction stories.

Although 'science fiction' was not a term in use, nor a genre when these authors put pen to paper, we as 21st century readers can identify the features that make a science fiction story. From the writing of the seven authors featured so far, I have discovered stories about time travel, journeys to other planets and parallel worlds, scientific inventions, aliens and fantastic creatures, and each story is written with intelligent and often satirical engagement with contemporary scientific debate and the state of the society the author lived in.

Scotland may not be the first country that springs to mind when you think of science fiction, but looking back into our history, it is actually no surprise that science, innovation and discovery have been such prominent themes in our literature. Scots are famed worldwide for their feats of engineering (there's a reason Star Trek's Scotty was Scottish) and numerous discoveries and inventions have come from Scotland – the television, the telephone, penicillin, to name but a few. As well as this involvement with the rational and logical, Scotland has ancient, deeply embedded traditions of religion, superstition, magic, and belief in other-worlds and faerie realms.

Scottish authors have not only participated in the tradition of early science fiction, but a few have been rather influential in developing the genre – the most obvious, of course, being Robert Louis Stevenson's *The Strange Case of Doctor Jekyll and Mr Hyde*. But there are also other authors, lesser known today, who were very well-known in their time, such as George MacDonald, author of *Phantastes* and *The Princess and the Goblin*, who is recognised as one of the fathers of the modern fantasy genre, who strongly influenced authors like C.S. Lewis (*The Chronicles of Narnia*) and Lewis Carrol (*Alice in Wonderland*). Andrew Lang was so prolific and popular a writer, that Irish playwright George Bernard Shaw once commented that "the day is empty unless an article by Lang appears".

As well as those once-famed and forgotten today, we have made some interesting discoveries of authors who you might otherwise have never heard of at all: May Kendall, who collaborated on a novel with Andrew Lang, and, it could be said, was a science fiction poet; Andrew Blair, a twenty-five-year-old doctor from Fife whose imagination for invention was absolutely astounding. Information on Blair is so scant that most of what I found came from digging into archives and finding his obituary in an 1885 edition of the *Dundee Evening Telegraph*.

In other cases, it has been fascinating to see the writers who are well known today in the literary world for other works, but have harboured an interest in science fiction. John Buchan's short story *Space* – unearthed by Paul F Cockburn for the first issue of *Shoreline of Infinity* – is a story about a physicist's search into invisible worlds. Lewis Grassic Gibbon's novel *Gay Hunter*, which features in this edition, is a thrilling tale of time travel and fascism. And soon in SF Caledonia, we'll uncover some stories of the occult from the creator of Sherlock Holmes, Sir Arthur Conan Doyle.

In each SF Caledonia article, I review the text honestly (not all of them translate well to modern readers), and place the book in its context and give a brief biography of the author. A short and sometimes abridged extract of the work is published too. My initial aim for this series was to find the earliest possible example of Scottish science fiction, but along the way I have been exploring as many stories as I can that can be considered to be the forerunners to modern science fiction. The earliest find so far has been George MacDonald's *Phantastes*, which was published in 1858. I hope to find older examples to see how far back science fiction goes in Scotland's history. But it is not a race to the end. It is discovering the stories themselves that is the prize, not how old they are. And this series so far has been full of surprises, and I hope to encounter many more.

Issue 1 – John Buchan, *Space*

Issue 3 – David Lindsay, *A Voyage to Arcturus*

Issue 4 – James Leslie Mitchell (Lewis Grassic Gibbon), *Gay Hunter*

Issue 5 – George MacDonald, *Phantastes*

Issue 6 – Andrew Blair, *Annals of the Twenty-Ninth Century*

Issue 7 – Andrew Lang and May Kendall, *That Very Mab*

Coming soon… Issue 9 – Robert Ellis Dudgeon, *Colymbia*

Extract from SF Caledonia, Shoreline of Infinity 4:

Lewis Grassic Gibbon and his celebrated trilogy, A Scots Quair, *enjoy their place in the spotlight, but the unique SF canon, published under his birth name, James Leslie Mitchell, go virtually ignored and unstudied by academics. It's time we gave Gay Hunter some attention.*

So what is it about? Don't be confused by the title. Gay Hunter is the name of the protagonist: a young American archaeologist, visiting London for an academic conference. At the start of the story, by the roadside, she encounters a very unpleasant Fascist man, Major Ledyard Houghton, and offers him a lift in her car. That evening, Gay despairs to find that they are checked into the same hotel, and they end up being seated together at dinner. After quarrelling over their respective ideologies, and the Earth's future fate, Gay challenges him to try an experiment taught to her by her father, to peer into the future. This experiment is based on a real life theory of time and the power of the sleeping mind to enable time-travel, by J.W. Dunne in his book An Experiment with Time, published in 1927. Gay and Houghton make a pact to try the experiment that night.

Gay did not expect it to work. She is horrified to find that she has not only glimpsed at the future in her dreams, but has travelled bodily through time. She wakes up, naked and alone in a world given back to nature so completely that it seems like the ancient, primitive past. Gay is alarmed to find herself in an era far into the future, long beyond the aftermath of a nuclear war that tore the world to pieces.

Gay Hunter

(extract)

James Leslie Mitchell (Lewis Grassic Gibbon)

She looked round the room and its sham antique oak, all solemn lines of fiddley curlicues. A great sloped mirror showed herself. Being still very young, she looked at that self with attention, but not too much. The room was deserted but for the waiter bringing the soup. Then she saw Houghton enter.

He had changed from hiking-dress – perhaps he had carried that lounge suit in the rucksack. It certainly looked a trifle crumpled. And as certainly it improved his appearance. Gay drank soup and looked at him with a faint interest – he had good shoulders and a straight back, and the cool hauteur and rangy straightness of the English Army officer of myth and rumour. As good almost as meeting an ancient Mayan in the flesh.

Funny how much better the lounge suit was than the hiking-shirt and shorts. But she'd thought that often of the feeble attempts at

Art: Monica Burns

rationalisation in clothes that men and women made. The scantier the garments, the more feeble and ridiculous and lewd the wearers looked. The Victorians were perfectly right and logical, bless their padded bottoms. Either you clothed yourself or you went naked. To sling shorts or the various pieces of a bathing suit over this and that portion of your anatomy was to make those portions suspect and taboo…

Houghton was standing beside her. He was stiff. "I understand the waiter would like us to share a table and save him work. Lazy old devil. Do you mind?"

Gay shook her head, eating tepid fish. "I don't think so." She turned away her eyes from another fasces badge, in the lapel of the lounge suit collar this time. "How's the headache?"

He sat down, half in profile. It was a stern, good, absurd profile. "Gone for the time being; but no doubt it'll come back… No, damn you, I told you I didn't want soup. A chop, man."

This was to the waiter. He shook a little, old and servile. Gay gently restrained herself from flinging the remains of the tepid fish at the correct, absurd profile. She had often to restrain herself over bodily assault in matters like that. The damned horror of any animal addressing another like that! Then she saw the twist of Houghton's face. Poor idiot.

She said: "There's a stunt in sleep-making that my father and I used to use when we went digging down in Central America. Ever hear of a man J. W Dunne?"

"Eh?… No."

"He's not a quack doctor or a psychoanalyst. He wrote a book called *An Experiment with Time,* and Father got hold of it. If you develop the trick you can get to sleep quite easily – unless you grow too interested in tomorrow morning."

"Oh."

But Gay was not discouraged. It was two or three years since she herself had tried those experiments at the edge of sleeping to peer into the doings of the next day or so. Father had given it up. He had said it was dangerous without elaborate precautions – funny father, the sternest and best of materialists! – salt of the earth, the materialists, though there *was* all this half-witted outcry against them these days from the sloppily superstitious Quakers who masqueraded as physicists…Well, this was how…

The old waiter sighed, peering round the edge of the door. That young 'un from America was at it with the gentleman. Bit sharp, the gentleman, but you supposed he couldn't be blamed. You were getting old, and a bit deaf, though it made you run cold to think of that, and that the boss would get to know… He looked again. Still at it, she was.

Houghton said, "Sounds rubbish. How can you look into the future – into a time that doesn't exist?"

Gay shrugged. She was a little bored herself, by now. This bleak militaristic intelligence always bored her – made flirting with ship officers and gendarmes impossible. Kind of people who never thought of the thrill of a kiss as the moment before lips touched, but just the contact and crush and a greedy suction… "The point seems to be that events don't happen. They're waiting there in the future to be overtaken."

He said "Rubbish," again grumpily; then jabbed at his chop and was suddenly loquacious.

"By God, there would be something worth while if one *could* have a glimpse of the future – project oneself into it for no more than a blink. All this modernist botching of society and art and civilisation finished, and discipline and breed and good taste come into their own again. Worth while trying half a night of sleeplessness to see that."

Gay had been about to rise and have her coffee on the verandah; but now she could not, looking at him with bent brows.

"Is that what the future is to be?"

"Of course it is. Service, loyalty. Hardness. Hierarchy. The scum in their places again." His face twitched. "England a nation again."

"And beyond that?"

"What would there be? Some dignity in history; the national cultures keeping the balance…"

Gay whistled. "Poor human race! Is that its future? Well, whatever's awaiting it, I know it isn't that."

"Some Amurrican Utopia instead, with every nation denationalised and the blah of your accent all over the globe?"

"That's just rudeness."

He coloured, stiffly. "I'm sorry."

Gay said: "Even tomorrow won't show a glimpse of anything as bad as that. Or beyond it. If we sat down tonight and tried to glimpse the future, we'd find most things we expect haven't happened…"

"All right. Let's put it to the test tonight, according to the formula of this chap Dunne that your father developed. Lie and try a glimpse into the future – and see if it's your Utopia or a sane history that the future's going to hold."

Gay said: "Of course that's just fantastic. You can see only a little of your own future – through a glass darkly."

He was holding his head again. He was really ill, Gay thought. He said, with the rudeness of pain and unease: "Afraid, like most softies, eh?"

Gay knew it was silly, but also the project was a little intriguing. She shrugged. "All right. Let's. But – if we manage to see anything at all – how are we to know when we compare results that each is speaking the truth?"

"I'm not a liar."

Gay nodded, rising. "Lucky man. Well, I'll be seeing you."

IV

The heat grew more stifling as the night wore on. Ascending to her room at eleven, Gay found the warmth swathing the place like a thick close blanket. "Like Coleridge's pants, in fact." Coleridge provided one of her gayest memories:

> '*As though the earth in thick fast pants*
> *were breathing*'

"Poor planet, how it must have perspired! And I feel a bit like it myself."

She took off her dress and step-ins and kicked off her shoes and sat with her hands clasping her brown knees, and looked out at the hot, stagnant night of the Wiltshire Downs. Below, she heard the old waiter closing up for the night, and the sound of heavy footsteps enter the room next her own. She thought: "The haughty Britisher with the headaches," and sat remembering their pact. The foolishest thing – especially as she didn't feel in the least in the mood for trying a neo-Dunne test to-night... She picked up the newspaper she had brought unread from the smoking-room and opened it and began to read. The night went on. At midnight she heard the clocks chime below, and woke to the lateness of the hour with a little start:

What a world! Hell 'n' blast, what a world! – as Daddy used to say in moments when it vexed him overmuch. The cruelty, the beastliness, the hopelessness of it. Not for herself – she stretched brown and clean, and looked down at herself and liked herself and thought of her lovely job among the remains of the Antique Americans and her plan for a couple of babies, not to mention a father for them, and for reading a million books and seeing a million sunrises. But she was only one, and a fortunate one... All the poor folk labouring at filthy jobs under the gathering clouds of war and an undreamed tyranny – what *had* they to live for? Even she herself – would she always escape? Unless she hid from her kind in the busy world of men, sought out some little corner and abandoned life like the folk at Rainier, like the hermits of the Thebaid. Those children of hers – would they escape the wheels and wires of life any more than the children of others? Or their children thereafter, and so on and on, till the world was one great pounding machine, pounding the life out of humanity: making it an ant-like slave-crawl on an earth turned to a dung-hill of its own futilities. She thought of Houghton next door – he was more than Houghton, he was the brutalised and bedevilled spirit of all men, she thought. And for them and their horrific future they expected women to conceive and have fruitful bodies and bear children...

Suddenly the night outside seemed to crack. Sheet lightning flowed low and saffron down over Pewsey, lighting up the Downs, and flowing soft in the foliage of the trees. Gay went to the window and watched. The earth looked a moment like a sea of fire, as though that Next War's bombardments were opening their barrage. It was hotter than ever.

She got into her sleeping-suit, put out the light, and lay down with only a sheet covering her. So doing, the view of the night vanished, for the windows were high in the wall. She stretched her toes and put her right arm under her head in the fashion that always so helped her to sleep, and closed her eyes.

Half an hour later she had tried most positions conceivable and inconceivable. But the newspapers were haunting her from sleep. She got up and drank a glass of water – tepid water that seemed to have dust in it. Low down over Upavon the thunder was growling dyspeptically. She lay down again, throwing off the sheet this time, and lay open-eyed, staring into the darkness, young, and absurdly troubled, she told herself, a little whipper-snapper absurdly and impudently troubled over a planet that wasn't her concern… Except that she hated the thought of those babies of hers, in the times to be, coughing and coughing up their lungs as the war-gas got into them…

It was only then that she remembered again her pact with the Fascist, Houghton.

V

Dreams, and a floating edge of mist. (But you must not dream. You must stay just on the edge of sleep, concentrating. So that you might awake and jot down your impressions of the pictures.) She tried to rouse herself, but a leaden weight seemed pressing now on her eyelids. Yet again she told herself not to dream.

Outside the lightning flashed, forked lightning as she knew through her closed eyelids. But now the dream-pictures were mist-edged no longer, they were jagged like the lightning. She knew herself caught in a sudden flow of images she had never tapped before – slipping and sliding amidst them like a diver going over Niagara. Something suddenly snapped and the pictures ceased…

Bombardment. The sky burst and showered the earth with glowing meteors. Great-engined monsters roared athwart the earth. Tribes fled and hid in dim confusion and climbed out again to the burning day. Great temples rose to insane creeds, and gangs of red dwarfs laboured at titanic furnaces. Peace flowed and flowered with winking seasons, season on season. Then again the sky broke and flared with terror. Now faster and faster went her fall over and into an unthinkable abyss, in a wink and flow of green and gold and jet. Ceaseless and ceaseless.

Then something smote athwart the rapids, and the pit opened and devoured her.

2. The Incredible Morning

I

SHE OPENED her eyes and saw that it was not yet dawn. There was a pale light all abroad the great stretches of the Wiltshire Downs, forerunner of the sunlight, but only a ghost of its quality. A little rain was seeping away into the east. She heard the patter of its going, light-footed, through the darkness into the spaces where the east was wanly tinted. She sat up.

Close at hand a curlew called.

She was aware that she was still dreaming, for the window of the room in the 'Peacock' was set high in the wall, so that, lying in bed, as she lay now, she could see nothing of Pewsey or the Downs beyond. This was a fragment of night-time dream. Drowsy, she lay back again, cuddling her face in her arm, and reaching out her left hand to draw up the sheets about her. Her fingers strayed uncertainly, finding no sheet. With a sleepy irritation she sought further, and then sat up again. There was no sheet. But something else had led her to sit erect. Her hand had touched her own skin.

She was naked.

She put out her hand in the dimness and touched the bed. It was not a bed. She was lying on a bank of earth – a grassy bank. It was wet with dew. Her back and legs were wet and chilled with the dew. She sat erect, very rigid, her hands behind her.

The curlew called again, very close at hand. Wings flapped in the dimness, darkness-shielded, and there came a splatter of something in a hidden pool. Gay put up her hand to her mouth and bit it.

She gave a cry at the realness of the pain. What was it?

Where…?

Hell 'n' blast, she knew! Sleep-walking! Not that she had ever sleep-walked before, that she knew. But that was what it must be. She had got out of her room and out of the 'Peacock,' and wandered out to the country beyond Pewsey. What a mess!

She rubbed her chilled self and put up a hand to push back the hair from her forehead. Soon be quite light – probably not yet four o'clock. She must get back. With a little luck she might get back unseen. The labourers' wives would just be stirring to light their morning fires.

She stood erect; and instantly sat down, gasping. There was something strange in the morning air that caught at her lungs, icily as though she had swallowed a mouthful of snow. Now she became aware of another fact – the rate at which her heart was beating. It was pounding inside her chest, insanely, and the blood throbbing in her forehead with the rapid beat of a dynamo. Sleep-walking and nightmare – Oh, what a fool!

She sat with her head in her hands, giddy, till the world about her began to quiet into unquivering outlines. Her heart was easing to normal pulsations. Through her fingers she saw the dawn coming on Pewsey.

And there was no Pewsey.

II

She sat in a great dip of the Downs, grassy and treeless, houseless, without moving speck of life, that she could see, north, south, east or west. In the coming of the sun great hummocks at a distance shed themselves of shadows, they seemed like great tumuli as the light came upon them. A wind was coming with the light, and blew cold with dew. But it changed and grew warmer, blowing upon her naked body, blowing her hair about her face. Below the little incline on which she sat a stream that wandered through the great hollow in the Downs lost itself in a reed-fringed stretch of water: she saw that it was a marsh-fringed loch, stretching its reeds away to the foot of the tumuli.

She began to weep, terrified and lost, watching that bright becoming of the day. Hell 'n' blast, she was mad – mad, or in a nightmare still. Where was her room and her clothes and that report on Toltec pottery?

She closed her eyes, sticking them fast, gripping her head in her hands. Then she dropped them and opened her eyes. She gave a low cry.

A great beast had come snuffling up the hill from the reeds and stood not a yard away from her, gigantic in the half-light, with pricked ears and a drooling tongue. Its musk smell smote her like a blow. It had the bigness of a bear, though the shape of a wolf. It gave a low wurr and dropped one ear.

Gay screamed, piercingly.

At that the beast backed away, growled blood-curdlingly, then turned, clumsily, and trotted away. Gay watched it with a breathless disbelief as it entered the reeds. A grunt and yap emerged. The reeds ceased to wave and move. Gay's frozen silence went.

"Lost, lost – oh, I'm lost!" She screamed the words, knowing that someone would come and shake her awake and help her – the chambermaid, perhaps. She stared about her wide-eyed, waiting that coming. The day brightened and grew.

No smoke. No sign of a house or of human habitation. She raised her eyes to the east and saw against it a moving dot. It grew and enlarged, coming earthwards and nearer. She held her breath.

It was a great bird the size of a condor, and something of the same shape, with a crooked beak and immense pinions that beat the air with the noise of a river paddle-boat. It might have been twelve feet from wing-tip to wing-tip. It planed down close to the earth, to the spot where Gay stood and glared, uttered a raucous and contemptuous "Arrh," and wheeled up into the sky again.

A condor *in England!*

Gay began to talk to herself. At the first word the silence of the deserted countryside seemed to intensify, listening. Breathtaking and terrible.

"I don't care! This isn't real, but I won't go mad! I won't, I…" She realised she was dreadfully thirsty, her lips grimed as with ancient dust. She glanced down at her body and saw it the same, covered evenly as with a thin sprinkling of soot. With a desperate courage she looked towards the loch. The beast…?

She picked up a stone in each hand and ran down into the water. It caught her and almost choked her, deep. She dropped the stones and splashed and swam, gasping. Something in the water caught at a foot, slimily, but she kicked it away. When she swam back to the shore again and climbed, gasping, from the icy embrace of the water, and wrung that water from her hair and wiped it from breasts and body and legs, she felt as though she had sloughed more than the covering of brown soot-dust. Wiping the water from her eyelashes, she raised her head again, knowing that surely the icy dip would have restored her sanity as it had cleansed her body. Around her were the unfamiliar, treeless, uninhabited hills. Then she saw something white rising up from the foot of the incline where she herself had awakened. It elongated and stretched, cruciform-wise. It was suddenly rigid. It was a man, naked as herself, and staring at her with dazed and astounded eyes.

It was Major Ledyard Houghton.

III

Her first impulse was to turn and run. But that was one too ridiculous to follow. Absurdly, she remembered a story from some Victorian romance of the heroine, nude, discovered by a man, and the modest female covering her face with her hands to hide her *identity*…She giggled and sank down on the grass.

"Thank goodness there's someone else in this mess. But however have we got into it?"

"Damned if I know. I woke and saw you swimming down there… if I am awake."

"Don't worry about that. I've thought it all out for myself, and you can take the results on trust. But I do wish you'd sit down."

"Why?"

Gay clasped her knees with her hands. "So that we can talk. And you're rather – undraped." He had an exceedingly white skin. It turned a rich crimson, face, neck… Gay turned away her eyes, politely, from survey of its further possibilities. He slumped down in the grass.

"Oh, damn it!"

He leapt up again. He had sat on a gorse-bush. Gay put up her hands to her eyes and giggled helplessly.

Giggling, she heard him say, hardly, "If you've got hysterics, you can get out of them. I'm off to see what's happened."

He was. He had jumped to his feet again. He had broad shoulders and shapely hips, except for one with a great scar, like that of a branding-iron, across it. Gay stared at the scar, herself standing up. "Where can you go?... And where did that happen to you?" He stared over his shoulder, angry and ludicrous. "Eh? What? What happen?" He coloured again, richly. "War-time wound."

"I see. And where are you going?"

"To find..." he stared around, "some house."

"Does it look as though there are any?"

It did not. The fact seemed to sink into their unevenly beating hearts. It was a land wild and forgotten. No human feet had trodden it, or voices called here, or the busy world of men reached out a hand here for long ages. The sunlight ran its colours up and down the near hills, gay with gorse. Far off a peewit wailed its immemorial plaint. There was no mark of cultivation or sign of human kind. Gay said, very quietly:

"Something has happened to us. I don't know what. But we're here, lost, as though we'd been newly born. If we're going to search out anything, perhaps we'd best do it together." She shaded her eyes with her hand, looking towards the tumuli. Without much hope: "There might be something to help us in those mounds."

They set out, almost side by side, across the spring of the grass. In Gay's mind was a bubbling tumult of thought and speculation, backgrounded by a horrible fear which she closed away. That wouldn't help, she'd to keep sane; and keep up with the headache man; and be thankful she'd a decent figure under these shy-making circumstances.

She glanced down at it, nicely browned, and felt absurdly cheered. Houghton swung beside her in silence, his neat, thinned Greek profile rigidly towards her, his eyes fixed ahead. She suddenly realised that he was elaborately and painstakingly *not* looking at her. Also, that he was wishing, with an angry embarrassment, that she would not look at him.

They came in silence to the foot of the great mounds. There were three of them, matted in long, coarse grass. Gay went through the space between the nearer two and saw beyond merely such rolling hill-country, rolling deserted to the horizon's edge, as lay to the west. She heard Houghton breathing, coming round the corner.

"They're just hills."

Gay shook her head. "Mounds, I think. I've dug ancient ones in Mexico, and they've much these shapes, ruined buildings with a thousand years or so of the blowing of sand and earth on the top of them…" She stopped, appalled. "Oh, God!"

He barked, "Eh?" – it must have been his tribal war-cry staring about him. But Gay was merely looking blankly at the mounds. She said:

"I don't know much of the Pewsey country, but there were no mounds near the village last night. None marked on any archaeological map. If these have taken years to accumulate, then…"

For the first time their eyes met, and she saw herself globed in the light grey eyes of Houghton – shallow, puzzled eyes, faintly red-rimmed. She saw her face, strained and white, in that reflection, above her brown throat… Houghton looked away.

"Then this can't be the Pewsey district."

"But it is. That hill over there – I saw it as I went to sleep last night – if it was last night." She felt suddenly breathless and sat down. "Listen, what did you do when *you* went to bed last night?"

"What? Tried the formula of this Dunne rubbish you talked about."

"Did you have any success?" Gay's voice sounded far away to herself. "Stuff like nightmare after a bit. Half-dozing, I suppose. The lightning cracked into the stuff and made my headache twice as bad. Then I slipped into the stuff again – damned rubbish. Woke up and saw you."

"This rubbishy dream stuff – did you have a sensation of going at a tremendous rate – slipping over the brink of a precipice?"

He scowled in thought. "No. Something – like going up a spiral staircase, and lights winking in and out from the windows. Anyhow, what does it matter? What's it to do with this – blasted insanity?"

"I'm not sure – yet.' Gay Hunter still felt breathless. That, and queer, as though she was about to be sick. "But I've a guess – oh, hell 'n' blast, it can't be, it can't be!"

"All this is rot to me. Look here, if we're going together, we might as well start. I'm going on – to get clothes somewhere, and back to London, whatever has happened here in Wiltshire."

Gay stood up, slowly, a queer look on her face. "All right? East?"

"That's the direction of London, isn't it?"

"Yes, that's the direction of London. Or was."

"Eh?"

She gripped his naked arm. "What's *that?*"

That was a movement in the long grass at a distance of ten yards or so from the mounds – a movement that ended in a tall, blonde woman, unclad as themselves, with a scared, astounded face, rising into full view and staring at them with horrified eyes. Gay blinked her own eyes at the sight. Had the whole damn landscape been showered with undraped females in the night? O Lord, she was going mad…

"*Ledyard!*"

Houghton stood halted, staring, a dismayed, agonised, smoking-room-story blush in effigy.

"Jane!"

Gay slumped down in the grass, too wearied with surprises even to giggle. "Do introduce us."

"Eh? What? Oh *Lord*, Jane!…This is Lady Jane Easterling, Miss Hunter."

Monica Burns is the Assistant Editor and First Reader at *Shoreline of Infinity*. She is also a writer, comics artist and perpetual student, soon to finish her second Masters degree at her third Scottish university.

THE BEACHCOMBER PRESENTS
MUTABLE MARTIANS
AH – HOW LOW THE MARTIANS WERE LAID...
AND ALL BECAUSE THEY WANTED SO MUCH TO BE GOOD NEIGHBOURS.
IT ALL BEGAN IN THE ANCIENT PAST. THE MARTIANS, A NOBLE AND
ADVANCED RACE BEGAN OBSERVING THEIR NEIGHBOURS ON EARTH.
ΑΡΗΣ
BEHOLD HOW THESE TERRANS WORSHIP OUR WORLD.
WE MUST BE CAREFUL NOT TO CONFLICT WITH THEIR BELIEFS.
THEY REACT BADLY TO OPPOSING VIEWS.
DOWN THE CENTURIES, THE MARTIANS ADAPTED THEMSELVES TO HUMAN EXPECTATIONS, FEARFUL OF THE CONSEQUENCES SHOULD THEY FAIL.
THIS WAS HARD ENOUGH IN AN AGE OF MYTH BUT IT WAS MORE DIFFICULT WITH THE DAWN OF SCIENTIFIC SPECULATION.

IT ALL STARTED WITH GIOVANNI SCHIAPARELLI.
SCHIAPARELLI MADE THE BEST OBSERVATIONS OF MARS IN HIS TIME. HE MAPPED THE RED PLANET IN GREAT DETAIL.

THEN, IN 1877, HE MAPPED A NETWORK OF LINEAR FEATURES WHICH HE CALLED 'CHANNELS.' THE ITALIAN WORD 'CANALI' WAS MISTRANSLATED 'CANALS' IN ENGLISH AND SPECULATION BEGAN ABOUT THE CANAL BUILDERS.
CANAL BUILDERS ON MARS

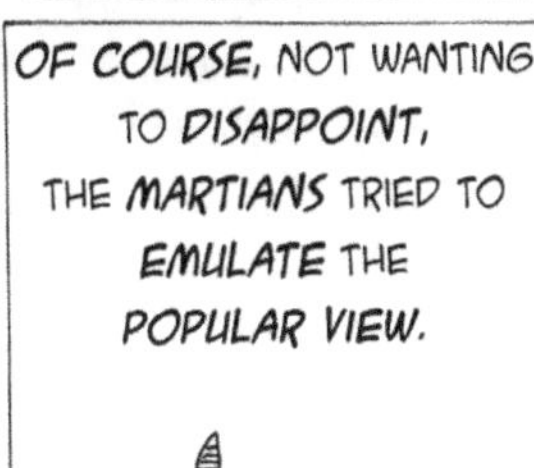

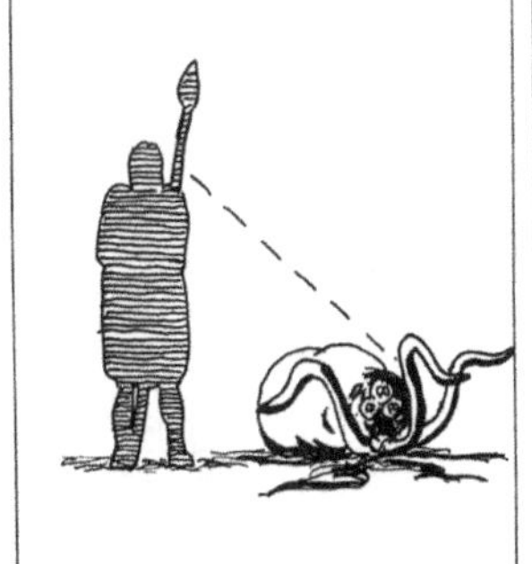

OF COURSE, NOT WANTING TO DISAPPOINT, THE MARTIANS TRIED TO EMULATE THE POPULAR VIEW.

THEY BUILT THE WAR MACHINES OF H. G. WELLS.

THEY WERE ALTOGETHER MORE GLAMOROUS IN THE TIME OF EDGAR RICE BURROUGHS.

THE 20TH CENTURY STARTED WITH A LOT OF INTERESTING IDEAS. MARTIAN FASHION JOURNALISTS COULD REPORT ON THE NEW FORMS THAT THE WRITERS AND ARTISTS OF EARTH WOULD DESIGN EVERY FEW YEARS.

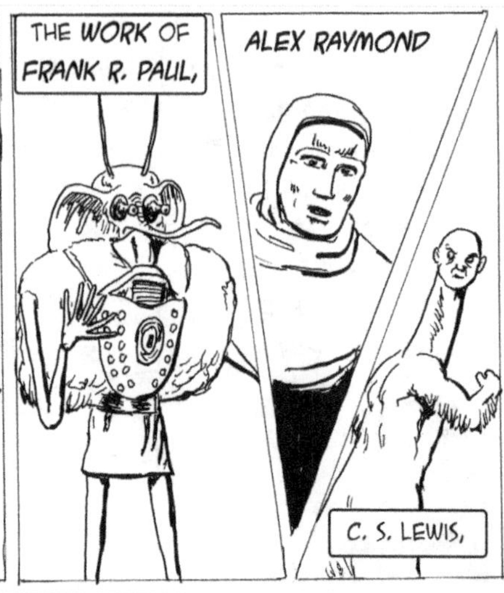

THE WORK OF FRANK R. PAUL,
ALEX RAYMOND
C. S. LEWIS,

CHUCK JONES.

HOWEVER THE FUN WAS TEMPERED BY A CERTAIN WISTFULNESS.
IN THE STORIES, EARTHLING HEROES VISITED MARS...

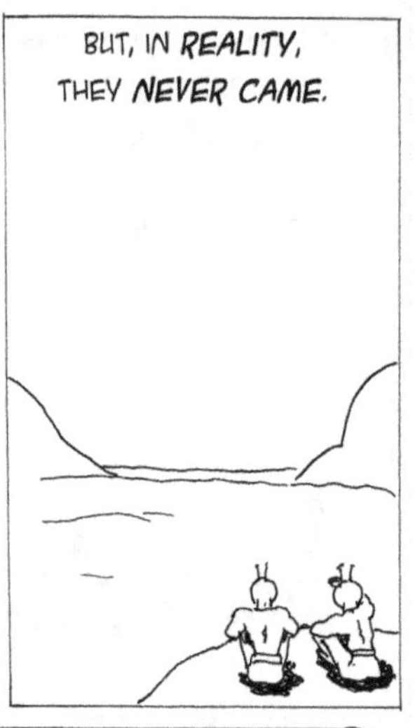

BUT, IN REALITY, THEY NEVER CAME.

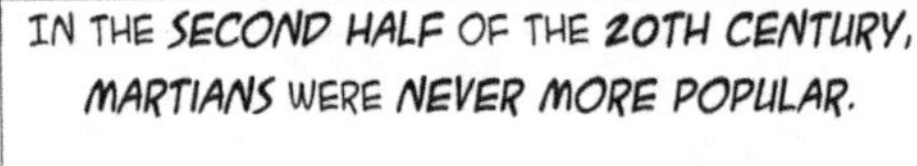

IN THE SECOND HALF OF THE 20TH CENTURY, MARTIANS WERE NEVER MORE POPULAR.
YET THE WEEKLY CHANGES OF FORM WERE TAKING THEIR TOLL ON THE HAPLESS MARTIANS.

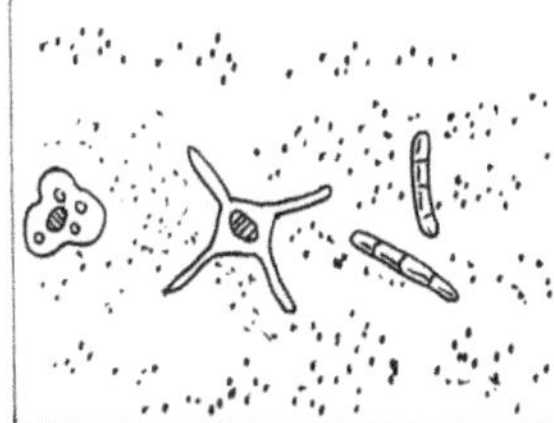

A MARTIAN LIST

H. G. WELLS 'THE WAR OF THE WORLDS'
EDGAR RICE BURROUGHS 'A PRINCESS OF MARS' AND MANY MORE
RAY BRADBURY 'THE MARTIAN CHRONICLES'
FRANK R. PAUL 'THE MAN FROM MARS' IN 'FANTASTIC ADVENTURES' 1939
ALEX RAYMOND 'FLASH GORDON'
C. S. LEWIS 'OUT OF THE SILENT PLANET'
CHUCK JONES 'DUCK DOGERS IN THE 24½ CENTURY' CARTOON SHORT
JOSEPH SAMACHSON AND JOE CERTA 'THE STRANGE EXPERIMENT OF DR. ERDEL' IN 'DETECTIVE COMICS' #225
WILLIAM CAMERON MENZIES 'INVADERS FROM MARS' FEATURE
STAN LEE AND JACK KIRBY 'THE JOKER!' IN 'AMAZING ADVENTURES #5
JOHN L. GREEN 'MY FAVOURITE MARTIAN' SITCOM
GEORGE PAL 'THE WAR OF THE WORLDS' FEATURE
BRIAN HAYLES 'THE ICE WARRIORS' TV EPISODE
GERRY ANDERSON 'THUNDERBIRDS ARE GO' FEATURE AND 'CAPTAIN SCARLET' TV SERIES

Imagining Positive Futures

Charles Stross

SF is written by human beings, and human beings are social animals; what we write reflects the zeitgeist, so when current affairs seem menacing our visions of the future turn dark and dismal. There's a little bit of lag in the system – it typically takes a year or more to write a novel, and another year to publish it, making novel-length fiction a truly terrible format for timely social commentary – but eventually the zeitgeist will out, hence the glut of horribly depressing near-future fiction that worked its way through the pipeline in the late 1970s wake of the 1974 OPEC oil price crunch.

Right now, expecting pessimistic futures is a no-brainer. In 2007/08 we had the global financial crisis, which was only partially addressed, followed by the counter-productive stupidity of austerity policies. The curious pathology of capitalism was identified by Piketty, whereby capital accumulates value faster than labour can, so that the rich get richer and the poor stay poor. We have rapidly accelerating climate change, which threatens to destabilize our food and water supplies. This in turn feeds political instability — the Syrian civil war and the Arab Spring were responses to regional food and water shortages (aggravated by the GFC) — with terrorism as a side-effect. And on top of that we appear to be witnessing the emergence of a global fascist/ nationalist movement, from Putin's Russia to Erdogan's Turkey by way of Trumpism and Brexit.

There are local problems as well. An entire generation of young people who can't aspire to home ownership or capital accumulation the way their parents could. An ageing population who increasingly require labour-intensive dementia care.

So it's no surprise that young adult fiction is dominated by dystopia this decade, or that near-future SF is increasingly gloomy. But what grounds for optimism are there?

Outside the developed (and particularly the anglophone) world, the picture is drastically different. India has a space probe in orbit around Mars and is rapidly industrializing; at the same time, the price of solar panels has fallen so sharply that the Indian economic build-up is moving to renewables. China, too, is prioritizing pollution and climate change above raw economic growth — and has developed dizzyingly fast over the past two decades. Africa, too, is developing economically, with an average growth rate of over 6% per year across the entire continent. If you're a citizen of what used to be called the Third World — the oil-fuelled Middle East aside — there's room to be optimistic about the future.

A decade ago, it looked unlikely that we'd ever wean ourselves off fossil fuels. Today, much political turbulence can be attributed to Big Carbon panicking and trying to hastily monetize their assets — coal seams and oil fields — before they lose all value because nobody is buying. Donald Trump has quit the Paris Accord but he can't stop solar power from undercutting coal on price, or car companies from switching to electric vehicles globally. Climate change is a major threat, especially to agriculture (which is largely oil-powered), but with ultra-cheap solar power, daylight spectrum LED lamps, and automation, we have the possibility of moving agriculture entirely indoors. The cost of access to space is crashing thanks to a generation of internet billionaires who are in competition to be the first to retire on Mars, and over the next decade networks of low-orbit satellites will provide cheap broadband internet access everywhere on the planet.

These are turbulent times, but doom is not inevitable or evenly distributed. It may be winter for the United States and the UK but it's springtime for Africa and Asia, where the majority of the world's population live. Even relative decline need not be absolute: Britain may not be a world empire today, but we're generally richer and healthier than our Victorian forebears. It doesn't take a miracle technology — working fusion reactors, molecular nanotechnology, AI — to give us the scope to write hopeful, optimistic future SF. It just takes a willingness to look beyond the short-term headlines and see the evidence that, for most people, things are actually getting better.

Charles Stross is the author of six Hugo-nominated novels and winner of the 2005, 2010, and 2014 Hugos for best novella, he has won many other awards and been translated into at least 12 other languages. He lives in Edinburgh.
www.antipope.org/charlie/   Twitter: @cstross

Tomorrow Never Knows

Iain Maloney

Charles Stross says in his piece on "Imagining Positive Futures"
that 'it's no surprise that young adult fiction is dominated by
dystopia this decade, or that near-future SF is increasingly gloomy.'
It is indeed no surprise: with the news full of death, destruction
and the rise of fascism, the present is bleak and the future far
from bright. But it's not just YA that's seen this bloom of terrifying
futures: Scottish SF in general has been producing its fair share of
near-future dystopias.

It should come as no surprise that this bloom coincided with
the 2014 Independence Referendum. The whole campaign –
whichever side you were on – was centred around one key
question: what do you think Scotland's future should be like?
The Yes camp included an energetic and vocal group of artists
who took two key skills into the campaign: a love of imagining
alternate possibilities, and an understanding that harsh economic
realities and a lack of guaranteed funding are not definitive
reasons for abandoning a dream. As Kathleen Jamie put it on BBC
Radio 4's *Start the Week* (March 7, 2016):

> "We all underwent our own Project Fear in our late-
> teens and early-twenties when people were saying *you
> can't be an artist, you must get a job, think of your pension*
> and we thought *I cannot live like that*, went on to become
> artists, grew in confidence and became successful. So it's a
> very small jump from that personal and private movement
> into saying to the whole nation *yeah, we can do this.*"

The No side's arguments leant heavily on pessimism, the risks
of an unknowable future – the implicit flipside of 'better together'

is 'worse apart' – and Project Fear portrayed a 21st century of economic desolation, food banks, closing hospitals, security threats and no resources to fight them.

Interestingly, dystopian SF set in post-Referendum Scotland breaks neither Yes nor No. In some, independence is a disaster, in others a timely untethering. Phil Miller's *All the Galaxies* (Freight, 2017) posits a second failed referendum followed by a break up of Scotland into authoritarian city-states blighted by terrorism and martial law. Dan Grace's *Winter* (Unsung, 2016) on the other hand imagines England descending into chaos and Scotland standing as a beacon of hope for refugees from the south. Rather than trying to fictionalise a political viewpoint (80,000 words is a long way to saying 'I told you so'), authors seem to have been fired up by the act of engaging with potential futures and this has fed into their work.

Ryan Vance, whose current work in progress *Absent from the Feast* is an eco-dystopia set in rural Scotland concerned with famine, denial and grief, agrees: "This story didn't, in fact, begin as a dystopia, but a spooky domestic drama." Its inspiration came from "a historical account of the medieval city of Strasbourg where, following a period of bubonic plague, religious upheaval and ecological collapse, the populace was gripped by a mass psychosis [...] the dystopia genre became both an explanation for this idea and a driving force to tell this particular story at this particular time."

Dystopian fiction tends to come along at times of slide, where society is on a relentless helter skelter. "I think they come from our traumatised collective human mind," says Miller. "The shocks – economic, physical, mental – of the Industrial Age. The feeling that everything is getting faster and more intense."

The form is an imaginative response to the question, 'what's the worst that could happen?' What Miller calls "a sober, sensible, pragmatic dose of worst-case-scenario." The recent television adaptation of Margaret Atwood's *The Handmaid's Tale* made a huge impact on viewers and commentators, with critics describing it as 'chilling' (Rolling Stone) and 'horrifying' (Indie Wire). That, of course, being the point. Even Margaret Atwood said to the *New York Times* in 1986, "I delayed writing it for about three years after I got the idea because I felt it was too crazy." That Trump was elected during production simply made it more relevant.

Another forthcoming dystopia is Vicki Jarrett's *Always North,*

a gripping story of memory, reality, software, shamanism and
a really big polar bear intersecting in unexpected ways. When
the journal of a ship's navigator from a 2025 oil survey in the
arctic ocean links to events twenty years later in the Cairngorms
where an embattled human race struggles to survive cataclysmic
flooding.

Like Vance, dystopia seems to have come into Jarrett's book
unbidden. "It wasn't until I started getting feedback on drafts of the
novel and someone used the word 'dystopia' that it occurred to
me that's what I'd done. Initially I was caught up with abstractions
about time, how that underpins memory and what we perceive as
reality, then with what all that might mean for my characters and
their world, the physical specifics of the 2045 world took shape
along the way, in the process of playing around with all of that."

Michael F. Russell's *Lie of the Land* (Birlinn, 2015) begins
from a similar premise to Miller's novel, where environmental
catastrophe is the excuse for governmental authoritarianism.
His protagonist Carl Shewan has escaped the clutches of a
locked-down Glasgow only to be trapped on the west coast. A
government sponsored electromagnetic surveillance field, that has
the power to render people unconscious, is turned on. Some –
including Carl – are safe but isolated, coping with survivors' guilt
and cabin fever.

Russell was keen from the start to write a dystopia:
"Armageddon has always fascinated me – it's said that we are just
four meals from anarchy and putting characters under this kind
of stress is a great way of seeing what they are made of, and what
happens to personal morality when the rules change, survival is a
struggle, and the enforcement of societal laws is removed."

Near-future dystopia can be a tricky line to walk. You want it
similar yet different, so that the fictional elements cohere yet stand
out. This can be a challenge when reality – or "this shitshow", as
Vance describes it – is dystopian enough on its own. "In the year
and a half since I started writing this book," he says, "history has
insisted on overtaking me."

So it made me wonder if dystopian authors view their work
as warnings or as thought-experiments. "As a reader, you want a
good dystopia to be more of a warning than prescient foretelling,"
says Vance.

Miller, on the other hand, believes that "dystopias are
nightmares that you write so you hope they don't come true"

though agrees that "perhaps they are like literary warning signs along the road: look how 'Orwellian' has become a word we all know."

However aren't we in danger of preaching to the converted? The people the warnings are aimed at – totalitarian regimes in the case of *1984*, Christian fundamentalists in the case of *A Handmaid's Tale*, upwardly-mobile pigs in the case of *Animal Farm* – won't be reading. Banning, yes, protesting, yes, but never reading.

"Maybe dystopias are doomed to a Cassandra-esque fate," says Vance. "But if I didn't externalise the fear in some way I'd become as unhinged as the people I'm writing about. I think it takes an optimist to write a dystopia – because if there's no hope, why bother?"

Miller seems less hopeful, which is perhaps why his novel not only features a dystopic Scotland but a demonic figure actively navigating this Hell-bound handcart. "Does anyone seriously expect the future to be better any more? […] The ice is not going to re-freeze, the plastic in the oceans is not suddenly going to disappear, wars will escalate, not go away, and thousands are drowning in the Mediterranean every year."

Jarrett has a more pragmatic attitude: "I think literature is part of a broader human conversation and there are clearly things we need to talk about. Talk, not preach or dictate – it's more about raising questions, creating space."

And all in the service of a good story. "Message fiction is all very well," says Russell, "but it has to take second place to the characters, their individual predicament and conflicts."

Whatever the future holds for Scotland, at least we can be sure to have some good books to keep us company on the journey. Philip Miller's *All the Galaxies*, Michael F. Russell's *Lie of the Land* and Dan Grace's *Winter* are out now. Vicki Jarrett's *Always North* was acquired by Freight Books and Ryan Vance's *Absent From the Feast* is there for any canny publishers to snap up. The future for Scottish SF, at least, is optimistic.

Iain Maloney is – amongst many other accomplishments – Reviews Editor for
Shoreline of Infinity

Shoreline Infinity's
EVENT HORIZON
Sci-fi Cabaret
prose, poetry and music
www.shorelineofinf
EVENT HORIZON
EDINBURGH'S MONTHLY SF FESTIVAL
NO SMOKING

Event Horizon: Shoreline of Infinity's monthly sci-fi cabaret

Russell Jones

Way back in 2015, the first issue of *Shoreline of Infinity* was about to hit our earthly realm. Now, I don't like to see a book fizzle into the world – it has to bang! So, rubbing my belly, I said to the *Shoreline* team: "It's a rocket, why don't we have a launch?"

And so we did! We called our night "Event Horizon" (it's the point of no return, once you're close enough). Live sci-fi poetry, short stories, music and bad SF jokes regaled the good citizens of Edinburgh, and we slurped a delicious (bespoke) alien cocktail or two, reminiscent of the Mos Eisley Cantina but with fewer deaths. The night went so well that people asked for more and, not wanting to disappoint, we complied. After all, resistance is futile, isn't it?

Our aim was thus: bring people together. Whether they were hardcore SF fans, or a bit wary of the genre, we wanted to build a community, to get people talking and laughing together. Since then, we've put on over 20 sci-fi events in Edinburgh, including at the Edinburgh International Book Festival and Hidden Door Festival. We've showcased around 60 writers and performers, 20 bands and musicians, and dozens of artists. We've also ventured further afield, launching books under the *Shoreline of Infinity* solar umbrella, attending comic-cons, sci-fi conventions and more.

Event Horizon has received rave reviews, but we've even more pleased to meet our audiences and make those all-important connections. And that's our story up to now. There's no other night like *Event Horizon*, so if you'd like us to run one in your town, to organize your SF book launch or simply share our secrets, please get in touch via www.shorelineofinfinity.com

Making Art on the Shoreline of Infinity

Mark Toner

From the beginning, we knew that *Shoreline* was going to feature art in a prominent way. It seemed that most of the competition either did not have a lot of illustration, or featured images lifted from the portfolios in digital galleries without connecting the artist to the story. Art was rare or was a mere embellishment.

So, when Noel Chidwick put out his call for writers to contribute to our new magazine, I put out a similar call for artists who wanted to illustrate this new SF for the 21st century. The initial responders to that call are rightly commemorated on page 103 of our first issue.

We attracted a lovely mix of fledgling illustrators (Becca McCall, Monica Burns, P Emerson Williams, Sara Julia, Alex Storer) more experienced artists (Bill Wright, Stephen Pickering) and the revered veteran,Dave Alexander.

That first issue was a fairly simple affair from the art director's perspective. We had envisaged a digital publication and didn't want to overload the older ebook reading devices. So there would be a colour cover to display on web stores and only monochrome illustrations inside. Noel, with his compositor's hat on, came up with the layout and I commissioned the illustrators and cover artist. This was fortunate because there was a lot of reading to do to select the stories for that one.

The design of our magazine developed over the next few issues. We offered a print-on-demand hard copy version as an option for more traditional readers and were surprised how good the sample copies looked. Subscribers liked the printed copy too and we looked again at our design in this light. Internal illustrations would remain monochrome to keep printing costs down but there were some style improvements to make. Number two saw the introduction of graphical headers for our regular features and number three marked the appearance of our in-house comic character, the Beachcomber. He was intended to introduce classic tales from the S.F. back catalogue, which is the reason for the E.E. "Doc" Smith primer. However getting comic rights for existing short stories is difficult for a new magazine just building its circulation. So the Beachcomber now introduces new S.F. comic book stories every quarter.

We continue to refine the look of our flagship magazine. There will be a fresh look coming soon. Also we plan other publications that will get their own distinctive looks too. Watch out for new book series, comics and graphic novels bearing the *Shoreline of Infinity* brand in the near future.

Mark Toner is co-founder and Art Director and of *Shoreline of Infinity*

Multiverse

Russell Jones

"The Thing I love About Poetry is its Ion Engine"[1]
An Introduction to Science Fiction Poetry

It's been almost two years since I propositioned *Shoreline of Infinity* with some science-fictional verse, and since then the poetry section of the magazine has gone from strength to strength. We've seen great work from universally recognised names such as Jane Yolen and Iain M Banks, and provided space to lesser-known talented writers from across the cosmos. Our poetry section has expanded, and we're getting set to launch an SF poetry anthology in the not-too-distant future. Watch this space!

If you've not heard of science fiction poetry, you're not alone. It's a little-known but surprisingly widely-written genre which spans back to the early 14th Century, or potentially even earlier. In his preface to the 2012 collection of UK Science Fiction Poems, *Where Rockets Burn Through*, Alasdair Gray describes how Dante's *Divine Comedy* "is based on a model of the physical universe developed by pagan Greeks and accepted for over sixteen centuries by all educated folk with scientific attitudes" and that Dante "added what many today think fictions" such as interactions between Satan and God, and the existence of Heaven and Hell. And Dante is by no means alone, with John Milton,

Emily Dickinson, Ralph Waldo Emerson, Marianne Moore, Robert Frost, Leonard Cohen and many more having put science and fiction into verse. Most science fiction poems aren't simply about ray guns and alien abductions, but how potential changes in science and technology can prompt us to reassess our position in the universe. Flash forward to modern day and you might be hard pressed to find a poet who hasn't written a science fiction poem, though they might not identify it as such or – not wanting to be labelled a nerd or a philistine – want to admit it.

So what does the genre have to offer? It's been over 50 years since C.P. Snow's lecture, *The Two Cultures*, which set out to explain that a division between the sciences and the humanities was potentially detrimental to human progress, that we ought to "break the pattern" into which we have "crystallised". In Professor John Taylor's 1976 lecture *Scientific Thought in Fiction and in Fact* he describes science fiction as "the art of making the scientific 'if' interesting". More recently still, Edwin Morgan, the late Scots Makar (or Poet Laureate of Scotland) stressed that it was the duty of the modern poet to examine modern life in all its forms, which included the potential impact of science and technology. He frequently did this through writing science fiction poems and bringing them to a non-sci-fi-fanatical audience. Science fiction poetry has the potential to explore what it means to be alive today, to re-examine the past and to think about life in potential futures. Its various crossovers in theme and theory lessen the gap between science and art by embodying them both. The 'good' science fiction poem can postulate about the "scientific 'if'" in a short imaginative space but also retain the complexity of thought and emotion gained through poetic form and device. And they can offer readers a darn good yarn.

If poetry responds to the concerns of our time then it cannot ignore our concerns for the future. Contemporary writers of science fiction poetry are drawn to this, frequently reacting with dystopian scenarios but also with poems that express a hope for the future that is gained through scientific discovery and a call for greater human compassion. The speculative nature of the genre often feels like scientific hypothesis, not working through absolutes or guarantees, but through a sense of intrigue. Charm and wit are also abundant qualities of the genre as poets explore narrative perspectives (human or otherwise) and challenge our expectations of theme and form.

Edwin Morgan once said that "the last refuge of the sublime is in the stars." Whether or not you've an interest in traditional poetry, the science fiction poetry genre has the potential to move beyond looking backwards. Its frequent use of unconventional narratives and its experiments with form and theme mean that it is truly an art form which crosses divides and beckons in new audiences with a new, or yet to be, age. We at *Shoreline of Infinity* are pleased to have it within our covers.

Jones, Russell, ed., *Where Rockets Burn Through: Contemporary Science Fiction Poems from the UK* (London: Penned in the Margins, 2011).

Morgan, Edwin, "A View of Things" from *Collected Poems* (Manchester: Carcanet Press, 1996).

Snow, C.P., *The Two Cultures and the Scientific Revolution* (London: Cambridge University, 1959).

Taylor, John, *Scientific Thought in Fiction and in Fact* in P. Nicholls, ed., *Science Fiction at Large* (London: Gollancz, 1976).

---

[1] The title of this article, "The thing I love about poetry is its ion engine" is taken from Edwin Morgan's poem "A View of Things"

Wittenberg: A Double Sonnet

Jo Walton

When studying philosophy,
At Wittenburg, a man can thrive
At least, that happened to these five
Quite different men, as you will see.
Let's contemplate them in the bar
Drinking, caught up in disputation
Before they made their reputation
One moment, as they really are,
First Brother Martin, quaffing ale
Lays out his views on simony
And how he'd like the church to be
Faith before works, the Holy Grail.
"The night is cold, the moon shines bright,
It's such hard work to set things right."

The Danish prince says "It's so odd,
As Pico says, that man's between
Angel and beast, as we have seen,
In apprehension, like a god."
Faust laughs and sighs, he'd wish that true
He buys another round, his dream
Is not of fame, as it might seem
But knowledge, to have power to do.
Quoting Agrippa, Frankenstein
Says "We alone have power of life!"
Martin says "Only with a wife,"
But Hamlet laughs "We're all divine! "
The fifth man yawns, gets up to go,
"Good night," they say, "Horatio."

The Grief of Apollo

Jo Walton

(In memory of Marcia Sherman. This poem is set in the universe of my Thessaly trilogy.)

So much to teach, but still so much to learn:
A starheart's fires, a symphony, a leaf,
The fierce fiery yearning leap of soul
Creating, understanding, joy to burn
To comprehend so much, to know it whole
Even the hardest thing to handle: Grief.

I spent eternity evading grief
With every strategy that I could learn
To keep it out of reach, my friends still whole,
Like readers who won't turn the final leaf
Although they know the library must burn
As if they could preserve it in their soul.

Mine is a glorious immortal soul
And so I was more sabotaged by grief:
When conflagration catches me, I burn.
And I had no recourse, was forced to learn
Mortals, ephemeral as any leaf
When she I loved was taken from me whole.

No moments of her left, her life was whole
Completed, gone, and though there was her soul
Whirling through Hades like a wind-blown leaf
I had to wait through hurricanes of grief.
I couldn't reach her, couldn't even learn
Why she had wanted me to feel this burn.

I am the sun, my nature is to burn,
As bright white day enlightens, shining whole
Illuminating all that helps to learn
And laying bare the secrets of the soul –
But not like this! Not smothered up in grief
Autumnal trees, that mourn for every leaf.

As time goes on, turning another leaf,
I found the revelation, why we burn.
For every mortal life must pass through grief
If we have loved at all, and to be whole
We have to dare to love, and from the soul.
This was the lesson that was hard to learn.

I love each dying leaf, each song, I'm whole.
I burn as bright as stars, and grow my soul.
Grief still remains the hardest thing to learn.

Jo Walton comes from Wales but lives in Montreal, exclusively in the first person.
I've published thirteen novels, with a fourteenth due out in Fenruary 2018, as
well as three poetry collections, a collection of blog posts and a short story
collection coming soon. I've written in most subgenres of fantasy and SF, and
won a bunch of awards, including the Hugo and Nebula for Among Others
(2011), the World Fantasy for Tooth and Claw (2003) and the Tiptree for My
Real Children (2014).
My plan is to live to be ninety-nine and write a book every year.

'Slight Mechanical Destruction'
Iain M Banks

Zakalwe enfranchised;
Those lazy curls of smoke above the city,
Black wormholes in the air of noontime's bright Ground Zero;
Did they tell you what you wanted to be told?
Or rain-skinned on a concrete fastness,
Fortress island in the flood;
You walked amongst the smashed machines,
And looked through undrugged eyes
For engines of another war,
And an attrition of the soul and the device.
With craft and plane and ship,
And gun and drone and field you played, and
Wrote an allegory of regress
In other people's tears and blood;
The tentative poetics of your rise
From a mere and shoddy grace.
And those who found you,
Took, remade you
('Hey, my boy, it's you and us knife missiles now,
Our lunge and speed and bloody secret:
The way to a man's heart is through his chest!')
– They thought you were their playing,
Savage child; the throwback from wayback
Expedient because
Utopia spawns few warriors.
But you knew your figure cut a cipher
Through every crafted plan,
And playing their game for real
Saw through their plumbing jobs
And wayward glands
To a meaning of your own, in bones.

The catchment of those cultured lives
Was not in flesh,
And what they only knew,
You felt,
With all the marrow of your twisted cells.

Iain M Banks was born in Dunfermline, Fife. He died in 2013 at the age of 59 leaving us a wonderful legacy of 27 books, 14 of them science fiction. Charles Stross wrote: "One of the giants of 20th and 21st century Scottish literature has left the building."

The Morlock's Arms

Ken MacLeod

The wasps are big this year, the meteors
green in the summer night. Our land
ironclads are far away, our flying-machines
visit atrocity on innocence. We do not care.
This is the World State. We're a planet now.

Our empire was the sun,
famine or fusillade its worst extreme,
its best a world that turned
on a war we fought, in the air.

And we're still here, in the light,
we Morlocks, we whose corpses
rotted conveniently in the cosy catastrophe,
we feckless, toothless proles, feral cattle
for whom entropy was never cool.

No Empire now, nor New Jerusalem,
no Modern Utopia. Only the streets
of Earth and England

and a sense of something about to happen.
Because we never went away
we will think of something
in our own time, gentlemen. Please.

Back in Time

Jane Yolen

".. . back to a time when only the stones howled."
- Louise Erdrich (The Master Butcher's Singing Club)

So we got out of our time machine,
set for the beginning of the world.
The whirr of the fans and dials finally ceasing,
we opened the locks and stepped out
expecting a brand new quiet Earth,
the only sound to be ferns uncurling,
the kind of green voice that whispers,
not like the noise of humans, who are never still.

I placed my foot on the nearest stone,
like any explorer ready to claim the land.
The stone began to howl, as if it knew
the future, could predict pillage, spillage,
the spoils of war; could foresee stones broken,
fracked, fractured, fallen. It gave voice to the silence,
made loud protest to the universe.
I withdrew my foot as if it had been a complaint,
and we took off again.

Perhaps the future was where we needed to be
not the past, with its howling stones,
with it fierce seers, with its knowledge.

Jane Yolen has been called the Hans Christian Andersen of America. She has written over 300 books, many poems (including SF poetry), won numerous awards including the Nebula (twice), and is a past president of SFWA (Science Fiction Writers of America). She splits her time between her home in Massachusetts and her house in Scotland.

The Human Guest

Marge Simon

The mating time was brief this year.
Our women sang notes like
floss on the wine-wind plains.

A human came who forced his seed
on Ala of the Yellow Eyes. We pretended
to be honored; we felt otherwise.

After, Ala wasn't the same.
She cut her marvelous hair
which had been dark and long
grown down below her legs.

She wandered off to the Darklands,
heavy with child and none to celebrate.
We mourn her fate. If she survives,
she'll raise his spawn alone.

She was the envy of us all.
When the child is born,
she'll burn his father's image
in the sands of our dead oceans.

The human sits on our sacred stones.
He preens his beard and leers at females,
with no more thoughts to waste on Ala;
he never even knew her name.

Come burrow season, we prepare,
sharpen our talons on caddo root.
When the freezing gales begin,
the human will demand sanctuary,
as his kind always does.

We will confirm his welcome
with the strewing of his bones.

Marge Simon lives in Ocala, Florida. Her works appear in publications such as *DailySF Magazine, Urban Fantasist, Silver Blade*. She won the Strange Horizons Readers Choice Award, 2010, the SFPA's Dwarf Stars Award, 2012, and the Elgin Award for best poetry collection, 2015. She has won three Bram Stoker Awards for Superior Work in Poetry and the Grand Master Award from the SF Poetry Association, 2015.

Travels through the Kuiper Belt

Shelly Bryant

I

comet
in irregular orbit
when seen from its star
and the inner planets

from beyond
its steps ordered
pulled by powers
too vast too distant

too subtle
for earth's instruments
to take measure
her intellects to grasp

II

born in space
                my frigid form
centuries passed, chemically inert
until at last my sun
                pulls me in close
its heat on my skin
thawing my icy core
my jets, ignited
light the night sky

Ridley Scott's Alien with Moth

Benjamin Dodds

ride   arrowhead
     slide across massive faces
  and hideous   limbs
     preen on white   upholstered
         bulkheads
      disappear   into
                         measureless space
                            during widescreen
                            establishing shots

  noiseless grey invader
observe   this late 1970s future
   in which astronaut miners
  foul rare air
with absurd cigarettes
   (we patiently await
  NASA's smoking phase)

give in to unassailable   attraction
  hold fast to strobing brightness
      and ride roughshod
over bright smothering nightmare
    until slow credits
trigger   houselight-rise

War species
Grahaeme Barrasford Young

when we have finished with our system
do you think we can wander freely

what makes breakers of worlds believe
their galaxy will want them near

where, in that case, will be an awful way
very few embarking will survive

who, entering occupied space
will have to make their choice

which we ancestors can only hope
does not make new neighbours ask

why black holes suddenly seem bright
through the darkness just arrived.

Benjamin Dodds (@coalesce79) is the author of Regulator (Puncher &
Wattmann Poetry, 2014).
His work has appeared in *Best Australian Poems 2014, Stars Like Sand: Australian
Speculative Poetry* and on ABC Radio National's *Poeticaprogram*. His current
project is a verse novel exploring the personal and moral boundaries of scientific
research.
https://benjamindodds.wordpress.com

Shelly Bryant divides her year between Shanghai and Singapore, working as a
poet, writer, and translator. She is the author of seven volumes of poetry (Alban
Lake and Math Paper Press), a pair of travel guides for the cities of Suzhou and
Shanghai (Urbanatomy), and a book on classical Chinese gardens (Hong Kong
University Press). She has translated work from the Chinese for Penguin Books,
Epigram Publishing, the National Library Board in Singapore, Giramondo Books,
and Rinchen Books. Shelly's poetry has appeared in journals, magazines, and
websites around the world, as well as in several art exhibitions. Her translation of
Sheng Keyi's Northern Girls was long-listed for the Man Asian Literary Prize in
2012. You can visit her website at shellybryant.com

Erstwhile editor, publisher and printer, **Grahaeme Barrasford Young** returned to
serious writing at the turn of the century. He is widely published. His collection,
Routes of Uncertainty (Original Plus), appeared in 2014.

Also published by

Shoreline of Infinity...

THE GALACTIC FESTIVAL

by

Paul Holmes

Shoreline of Infinity's master puzzler

New puzzles to take your brain to a higher level

Available from

www.shorelineofinfinity.com

and all good bookshops

£8.50 paperback

£3.50 for ebook (PDF)

The Folger Variation follows three interconnected lives across different strands of time.

"...a joyfully dystopian, fascinating and challenging book. There is a distinct risk you will get to like it."

Available in digital variations from www.shorelineofinfinity.com

Flash Fiction Competition for Shoreline of Infinity Readers

Visible from the Shoreline of Infinity Beach Hut HQ are these landscapes illustrated by Becca McCall (below) and Siobhan McDonald. Let these illustrations – singly or together – inspire you to create a story. We're looking for flash fiction, which we're defining as a maximum of 1,000 words.

Just remember, *Shoreline of Infinity* is a science fiction(ish) magazine, and your story must be science-fictional.

Prizes: £40 for the winning story plus 1 year digital subscription to *Shoreline of Infinity*. Two runners-up will receive 1 year digital subscription to *Shoreline of Infinity*.

The top three stories will be published in *Shoreline of Infinity* –

All three finalists will receive a print copy of this edition.

Also

The best stories submitted will be published in 2018 in an anthology, and each contributor will receive a digital copy and a pro-rata share of the royalties.

The Detail

Maximum 1,000 words.

Maximum 2 stories per submitter.

Deadline for entries: midnight (UK time) 30th September 2017.

To enter, visit the website at:

www.shorelineofinfinity.com/2017ffc

There's no entry fee but on submission you will be asked for a secret code word only obtainable from reading issue 8 of *Shoreline of Infinity*.

How to Support Scotland's Science Fiction Magazine

Become A Patron

SHORELINE OF INFINITY HAS A *PATREON* PAGE AT

WWW.PATREON.COM/ SHORELINEOFINFINITY

ON *PATREON*, YOU CAN PLEDGE A MONTHLY PAYMENT FROM *AS LOW AS $1* IN EXCHANGE FOR A *COOL TITLE* AND A *REGULAR REWARD*.

ALL PATRONS GET AN *EARLY DIGITAL ISSUE* OF THE MAGAZINE QUARTERLY AND *EXCLUSIVE ACCESS* TO OUR PATREON MESSAGE FEED AND SOME GET *A LOT MORE*. HOW ABOUT THESE?

POTENT PROTECTOR SPONSORS A STORY EVERY YEAR WITH FULL CREDIT IN THE MAGAZINE WHILE AN *AWESOME AEGIS* SPONSORS AN ILLUSTRATION.

TRUE BELIEVER SPONSORS A *BEACHCOMBER COMIC* AND *MIGHTY MENTOR* SPONSORS A COVER PICTURE.

AND .... OUR HIGHEST HONOUR ... *SUPREME SENTINEL* SPONSORS A *WHOLE ISSUE* OF SHORELINE OF INFINITY.

ASK *YOUR FAVOURITE BOOK SHOP* TO GET YOU A COPY. WE ARE ON THE *TRADE DISTRIBUTION LISTS*.

OR BUY A COPY *DIRECTLY* FROM OUR *ONLINE SHOP* AT

WWW.SHORELINEOFINFINITY.COM

YOU CAN GET AN *ANNUAL SUBSCRIPTION* THERE TOO.

www.ingramcontent.com/pod-product-compliance
Lightning Source LLC
Chambersburg PA
CBHW061257210726
48293CB00003B/1003